ZO AND THE FOREST OF SECRETS

ALAKE PILGRIM

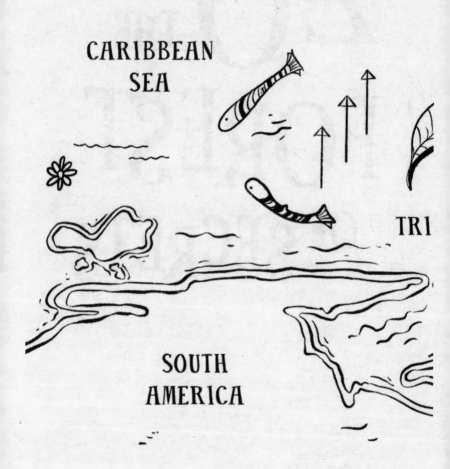

ZO AND THE FOREST OF SECRETS

ALAKE PILGRIM

KNIGHTS OF

Published by Knights Of

Knights Of Ltd, Registered Offices: 119 Marylebone Road, London, NW1 5PU

www.knightsof.media

First published 2022

001

Written by Alake Pilgrim

Text copyright © Alake Pilgrim, 2022

Cover art by © Tasia Graham, 2022

Set in Ovo Regular / 12 pt

Typeset by Marssaié Jordan

Design by Marssaié Jordan

Printed and bound in the UK

ISBN: 9781913311292

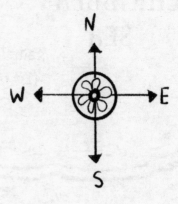

TOBAGO

NIDAD

N.E.
COAST

ATLANTIC
OCEAN

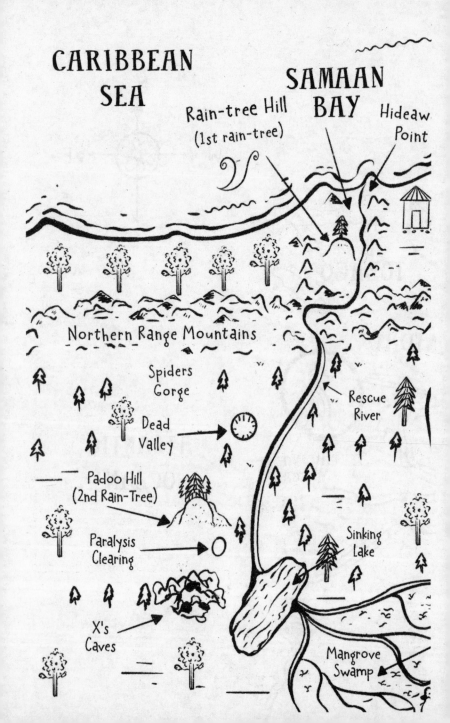

N

W E

S

The "Zoo"
(Global Research
Centre)

ATLANTIC
OCEAN

KEY

- Mountains

- Mangrove
  Swamp

- Forest

- Village

Yara's Garden

Transformation
Beach

Old Coral
Caves

ay

To my little one, for inspiring me to write this.
And to my family and friends, for sticking with me
while I did.

Chapter One

WARNING

Was the old man standing next to me crazy, or cool? I didn't have much time to decide.

Even in our heavy island heat, he was decked out in a three-piece multicoloured suit, with a floor-length coat made of scraps of fabric from every corner of the globe. To top it all off, he wore a straw fedora pulled low over his eyes, with a blue chicken feather dancing on one side.

"You better watch your back with that one," he muttered, interrupting my thoughts in a wheezy, almost laughing, voice.

"What?"

I inched away from him, nearly tripping over a speckled goat that, for some reason, was wandering the Samaan Bay market like a stray.

"Maaa!" it protested, rolling its eyes at me through wild tufts of hair.

"Sorry," I muttered.

Great. Now I was talking to goats.

"You will be sorry, if you don't get away from her."

Who was this guy talking about – the goat? Thankfully, it was already strolling away, not even bothering to look back at me. Meanwhile, the nearest vendor was at the other end of her stall, selling rough-skin lemons. She didn't have many customers. The rest of the market was loud and swarming with people, but this dusty corner was almost deserted. What crime did you have to commit to get stuck at a stall way out here?

Among the bones of old tents, shredded tarps and broken tables, the old man was strangely mesmerizing. He was lean, with a face full of dark angles and shadows. He wasn't looking at me. Maybe he wasn't talking to me at all. He seemed to be thoroughly inspecting a heap of bright orange mandarins, overripe in the sun, taking over the air with the smell of citrus and day-old roses.

I glanced around. Was no one else seeing this? Despite his get-up, nobody seemed to pay the old man any mind. I definitely didn't want to be the one staring with my mouth open, "catching flies" as Ms. Kofi would say.

Where was she anyway?

Ms. K, the woman in charge of my life here in Samaan Bay, was nowhere to be seen. She was probably still on the other side of the market haggling over the price of yams. She'd told me to get a bag of limes and come back to her quick sharp. But this was my first Friday market, and the most excitement I'd seen since moving to Samaan Bay the week before.

It was barely dawn, but the crowd in the rest of the market was as thick as ants on a pile of sweets. People had come from the surrounding villages to buy and sell their goods. For once, the half-dead village was pulsing and alive. In the crescent-shaped market, calypso, soca, chutney, reggae, dancehall, jazz, pop, afrobeats, filmi and gospel music blasted from the open stalls. Vendors sheltered under pink, green and blue tarps, chatting loudly over the noise, catching up on news, and selling everything from gru gru bef to underwear, saltfish to yard fowl, car parts, coconuts and "Cold-in-the-ice!" drinks.

Sweat stuck my t-shirt to my back. Somehow, I'd wandered out here, away from all the action.

A drink of water sounded great right now. I turned to go.

"Girl, listen quick, I don't have much time," the old man's voice froze me in my tracks.

"Mr. Yancy," a melodious voice cut in, "why you don't leave this child alone?"

The lemon vendor had just finished her sale and was staring at us suspiciously.

"You're Zo, right?" she asked, raising purple, pencilled-in eyebrows.

Apparently someone had sent my name out on the village hotline: look out for Zo Joseph, new to Samaan Bay.

"Why you don't mind your business, Miss Lady?" the old man snapped at her.

She puffed up like dough tossed in hot oil. "Who you calling Miss Lady?"

I backed away slowly. Why was I here at all? I should be with my dad in New York, instead of in Samaan Bay watching two strangers argue.

Da... I swallowed the lump that grew like a plum seed in my throat whenever I thought of him. Right now, he felt like a world away.

As the vendor and Mr. Yancy went back and forth, something caught my eye. My mouth dropped open in slow motion. Was this for real? The old man's coat seemed to change shape every time he moved. The patterns and colours shifted as if the coat had a life of its own. I looked closer. It was almost like it was rustling, moving, taking the shape of...my face.

I jumped back, choking.

"L-l..." My lips wouldn't move.

I shook my head and the coat stopped moving. It was still a crazy clash of cut-out materials, but that was all. I swung around wildly. No one near me seemed to notice anything strange. The old man and the vendor were still bickering, and she hadn't missed a beat. Clearly the heat was messing with my eyes.

"Listen, you!" the old man hissed at me suddenly, making me jump. "Do you see her?"

Under the hat, his eyes were golden-brown, glowing with a strange light.

"Wha-a-t?" I stammered.

The vendor quarreled about "mad people" coming to upset her day. The old man snorted at me. What on earth was he talking about? I could see the vendor-lady just fine. She was busy explaining to him, in no uncertain terms, that her name was Mrs. Boukan, not Toucan, and that she didn't appreciate his brand of nonsense at this hour in the morning. She was a powerful woman, with a stubborn smile and a bright blue headdress tied high above her forehead like a bird in flight. He'd be better off leaving her alone.

As for me, limes or no limes, I needed to get away from here and back to Ms. K.

Too late. There was Ms. Kofi, pushing her walking stick through the crowd on the other side of the field and limping hard in my direction. Now I was in real trouble. Time to go.

The old man spotted Ms. K too. He turned back to me, and for a second his face stopped me cold. Somehow, he seemed more scared than I was. He looked wild and... hunted.

"You don't see her?" he asked again desperately. "I know you can. You better wake up and use it before they do!"

What was 'it'? Who were 'they'?

Before I could move, he lunged forward and tapped me once with his index finger on the crown of my head.

"Hey!" I protested, ducking away.

"Wake up!" he hissed.

"Ay!" the vendor shouted. "Leave that child alone!"

She batted at him across the table, scattering her fruit.

He ignored her, pinning me in place with an acid stare.

Suddenly, a cloud of red dust swirled around me. I sneezed, seeing stars.

When I opened my eyes, the vendor was re-stacking mandarins, sucking her teeth and muttering. "Utter foolishness..."

Ms. K was headed for me with a face like rain.

And the old man was off in the distance, speeding away, with his coat flapping behind him.

Chapter Two
ESCAPE

Ms. K stalked ahead of me through the market, jabbing her walking stick in front of her like a sword.

"What was that old man telling you?" she probed again.

"Nothing," I said innocently, "he was just babbling."

The truth was, I had no clue what the old man meant, or why he was so afraid of Ms. K.

But I should've expected something like this. From day one, Jake, my mum's new husband, and the one who'd dragged us here to Samaan Bay, kept trying to tell me that this village was special.

According to him, it brought together traditions from Native peoples, Africa, India, China, the

Americas, Western and Eastern Europe, the Middle East, and more. People who, ages ago, had drifted or fled ("Or been taken hostage," I'd muttered) to this tiny corner of the world.

Every time I complained about being here, Jake had just flashed his superhero smile and said, "Trust me Zo, you'll see!"

Now, if by special, he meant that this place was spooky and weird, then after my experience in the market, I would have to agree.

I looked over at Ms. Kofi stomping along beside me. Why had the old man and his coat been trying to warn me about her? And how on earth did that coat have a life of its own?!

And most importantly, I hoped that the drama at the market hadn't made her suspicious about my morning plans.

Back at the stall, the vendor had only calmed down after I'd bought two large heaps of lemons. All she told Ms. K was that Old Yancy had been bothering me and that she'd chased him off.

The noise and smells of the market fell away, as Ms. K and I walked along the gravel road that led from the village to the smelter where I was supposed to meet Jake.

The road was deserted except for the occasional stray dog, dashing into the bushes on the side of the road.

Ms. K squinted at me with her sharp black eyes. "Well, next time, stay away from Old Man Yancy eh! He is walking trouble."

"Yes Aunty." I'd already figured that out.

Technically, it was my business what he'd told me, but I didn't dare say that out loud. Ms. K didn't take rudeness lightly. She was a bent woman, not much taller than me, with skin creased and leathered by years in the sun and eyes that shone like her gold hibiscus earrings. Despite her uneven walk and small frame, Ms. K was not one to play with. She was strong enough to carry the crocus bag of produce we'd bought on her head, laughing at my offer of help.

Right now, I needed to stay focused. I couldn't let that madman, and whatever issues he had, slow me down. So far, things were going according to plan. I'd gone to the market with Ms. K, giving Jake enough time to leave for work. Mum and the Terror were back at the cottage, about half a mile outside of the village.

Tayo, Jake and Mum's new baby, was mind-blowingly cute to the rest of the world. But to me he was the Terror, because, between his night-time screaming and daytime pooping, he was the boss of the house and he ruled with a tiny, iron, milk-covered fist.

He and Mum were probably still asleep – worn out from a night of feedings and nappy changes.

This was my chance. I had to get going if I was going to make it.

"Jake's giving me the grand tour of the smelter today," I reminded Ms. K, feeling a twinge as the lie slid off my tongue.

"Mm-hm." She adjusted the green and gold skirt wrapped around her waist without missing a step. "You have your food?"

"Yes, thank you," I smiled sweetly, hoisting the pack of supplies further up on my shoulders.

Good, we were back on track.

Ms. K clicked her tongue. "And no swimming by yourself. You hear me? Unless you want to end up like those people."

I rolled my eyes on the inside. Here we go again. At least I'd gotten her to stop asking about the old man. Now it was time to hear "don't go into the water by yourself", for the thousandth time.

Samaan Bay was still buzzing about the family who'd gone missing weeks before we arrived. They'd been on holiday in a village nearby. The parents had driven over to Samaan Bay and rented a speedboat to sail out to one of the coves beyond the eastern peninsula. Just after dusk, a fisherman had raised the alarm. He'd found the boat overturned past Hideaway Point, floating like a giant leatherback turtle.

The Coast Guard and Army had come looking for the family, with no luck. They'd even led search parties into the forest on Hideaway Point. But this was the northeast coast of Trinidad. As much as people might call it a small island, it was impossible to fully cover all of the forest, hills, and coves in this area.

Down on the village beach, I'd seen the rosaries, candle stubs, conch shells and deyas, smoking sticks of incense, coils of wooden mala beads, and fluttering prayer flags on thin bamboo poles, left behind by the villagers. Faded pictures, hung by relatives and friends from a twisted almond tree, spun in the sea-breeze. Scattered pieces of tinsel were all that remained of glittering tadjahs – small replicas of domed tombs – that had floated out to sea on the last night of the festival of Hosay, during which people had prayed for the missing family.

None of it had helped.

"No sign of them since," Ms. K cut in, as if reading my mind.

People decided that their boat had hit a bad wave and capsized.

"The sea is a jealous one," Ms. K warned me, her canerows plaited in a silver crown around her head. "She don't like to give things back."

A cold breeze from nowhere ran down my arms.

"I'll stay away from the water," I agreed.

I didn't need to hear that story again.

Why was I even here? I missed my old house and life in the city. Back home, swimming and gymnastics camps were going on without me. I was missing the holidays with my friends. I missed Da. He had made Samaan Bay bearable when he came to get me settled in, but once he left, that was it. This village on the northeast coast of Trinidad was far away from everything, backed by forest and mountains, trapped between two peninsulas that stuck out like arms on either side of a long, crescent bay. All around us was the sharp smell of the sea, but the rocky shore wasn't even great for swimming.

Instead of golden beach, abandoned fishing boats lined the stony sand in faded red, gold and green. Too many trawlers in other parts of the sea, rubbish, and oil spills had done their part. Most of the fish were gone from Samaan Bay and I wished we were too.

At least now I had a plan to get out.

I looked at Ms. K barrel along at a breakneck pace, despite the limp in her left leg. Operation Escape was in motion, and she didn't suspect a thing.

On my right, the sea winked at me from its shield of coconut trees. I grinned back. It breathed salty air into my face and surrounded me with the rushing sound of the surf, breaking on rocks again and again. On my left, on the other side of the potholed road, was the forest, with tracks leading up into the mountains. The village was behind us, out of sight.

"Swung right out of the belly of the whale and I never get weary yet!" Ms. K sang hoarsely as we walked. Her gold-capped teeth flashed in the sunlight. Her face was a map of crisscrossed lines, weathered by years on the beach cleaning fish, back when there were fish in Samaan Bay to be caught.

Soon, as the road climbed, she stopped singing.

We went higher. The sea dropped below us on our right.

"Aunty, let me take the bag. Please."

She waved me away, her breath sharp, face drenched with sweat.

I felt a stab of guilt. Ms. K had her own problems, and my plan wasn't going to make her life any easier. I tried to swallow my discomfort. In the end, it would all be worth it.

Suddenly, Ms. K stopped and so did I. The road ahead wound sharply up a cliff. The smelter, ringed by a concrete wall, was at the very top, its entrance hidden by trees.

"Ms. K, I've been here before," I pleaded. "You don't have to climb up."

She looked up at the steep slope and took a deep breath.

"Fine... but stick to the road!"

"Yes Aunty!" I turned to go, hiding my smile.

Ms. K muttered after me. "You know, that family was strange. The ones who went missing... They all had shaved heads. Even the woman. Pretty she was. Bald just like her husband and son."

"Yeah, weird," I said over my shoulder as I turned to go.

I'd heard this detail picked over by every one of the

15

village aunties, who kept the gossip wheel turning day after day.

"Lila and Sarun Khan and their one child," the old women tsked, shaking their heads. "I hear she was sick or something, but the sea have no mercy! Believe me..."

Ms. K cut through my thoughts, snapping me back to the foot of the road that climbed up to the smelter. "Listen, you go straight to your dad, you hear?"

I felt my whole body stiffen. It was a good thing that she was standing behind me and couldn't see my face.

"Jake isn't my...!"

She stuck her heavy staff on my shoulder, cutting me off mid-sentence. I spun around and froze.

In Ms. K's place was a hairy bristling creature, with four sets of shiny black eyes. Beneath its eyes were sharp claws on either side of a dark mouth. They opened as if in a smile. The staff on my shoulder was held in a long, pointed leg, covered with quivering hairs. It was one of eight legs curving from the vast golden body that blocked my way. I couldn't blink, move or breathe. The giant spider glinted at me.

"Stop..." it rumbled in Ms. K's gravelly voice.

The old man's warning rang in my head: "Don't you see? Watch your back with her!"

Before I could move or scream, Ms. K the spider touched the staff gently to my head. There was a flash. I saw nothing but light. An electric jolt went right through my body.

I opened my eyes to find Ms. K staring at me with a worried look on her face.

I found myself nodding. What had she been going on about this time? Head straight to Jake's office, don't swim in the sea. Strange. Something else had just happened, something that I should probably remember, but it fell from my mind like a short burst of rain. I wasn't sure why but, suddenly, leaving didn't seem like such a good idea.

"You alright?" Ms. K was staring at me as if I'd been hit in the head. She adjusted her checkered skirt and balanced the crocus bag on her head with one hand.

How long had I been standing here?

"You sure you want to do this today?" Ms. K offered. "I will call your da... I mean, Mr. Lee, and tell him you not coming again."

I shook my head slowly. It felt as heavy as a bowling ball.

Ms. K put both hands on her hips, her black eyes piercing mine.

Finally, she shrugged. "Okay."

I felt relieved and confused at the same time. For a second, I wasn't sure which way to go.

I forced myself to take slow steps on the road ahead. What was wrong with my feet?

I tried to wave. "See you later!"

"Mm-hm," Ms. K grunted, turning away.

My throat was dry as I stumbled up the steep path. I made myself walk calmly. When I looked back, Ms. K was already out of sight on the winding road that led back to the village.

Now that she was gone, I moved quickly. Excitement fluttered in my chest. There it was among the trees, snaking left from the road to the smelter - a half-hidden trail leading up into the mountains.

I took one last look behind me, to make sure I was alone, then slipped into the cool of the forest.

Chapter three

FALL

Something stung me in the neck – a small, sharp stab of pain. I slapped my skin and looked down. On the ground was a tiny silver creature like a gnat, with a bright green light, flickering out. It beeped like some sort of robot, then was still. I stared down at it. The forest had all kinds of stinging and biting insects, but I'd never seen this one before.

I looked around me slowly. It seemed to be the only one. That was a relief... It wouldn't do to walk into some kind of wasp's nest out here on my own. I dusted my hands and looked up at the hill in front of me.

Rain-Tree Hill was one of those places that felt like it was awake, watching to see what you were going to do. It stared down at me and my insect bite. I stared back more bravely than I felt.

Hours of trekking through the forest had finally brought me here. I sucked in the moist, earthy air. The hill was just like I remembered it from my hike with Da, back when he'd helped us move to Samaan Bay. I decided not to think about the day he left.

I took deep breaths, trying to shake the creepy feeling of being watched.

This place was strange, to say the least. Everything behind me was damp and forested, but ahead of me was a huge circular clearing and in the middle of it, Rain-Tree Hill. Somehow, in the rainy season, and in the heart of the forest, the hill and the ground around it were dry and bare, as if a fire had just passed through. Just like the ground that surrounded it, the hill was as naked as a vulture's head. It was a rectangular slab of red rock, sticking up from the surrounding valley.

As I moved toward the hill, I stepped off the leafy forest floor onto dusty gravel that crunched beneath my feet. Stevie Wonder's voice blasted from my headphones. It helped calm me down. Da was a huge fan. I pictured my dad's beaming face, covered with his bristly black beard and spiky moustache. I could see his dark, smooth skin, the wire-framed glasses that perched on his flared nose, and the high cheekbones that crinkled his eyes every time he smiled.

This whole elaborate plan was for him. It had better work.

From this close, I couldn't see the top of the hill, but I could get a sense of the odd table-like shape that had caught my eye when we first drove into Samaan Bay. I stepped slowly towards the tower of red stone and ran my hand across the surface of the rock. The stone was warm, covered with deep lines in different shapes.

"Indigenous hieroglyphs," Da had whispered when we were here, "pre-Columbus. Exact origin unknown."

"Why are we whispering?" I'd whispered.

He'd grinned and poked me in the arm. "You tell me."

Somehow, this felt like a place that liked quiet.

Da and I had talked under our breath about hieroglyphs and what the carved images might mean. They had come up on our trips before. After all, it was Da who took me hiking and camping all over Trinidad, from spotting red howler monkeys in the Nariva Swamp to the burping mud volcanoes of Piparo.

Every July-August holiday, when he was back on the island, Mum got to focus on her next exhibition, while Da and I went roaming.

We'd be setting up the tent in some deserted place when he'd ask: "What happened to the frog when his car shut down?"

"He got toad!" I'd roll my eyes and groan.

Yup. Dad jokes are a menace.

Still, he made me laugh. At least, he used to.

Now, I pushed those thoughts away and ran my hands over the markings on the side of Rain-Tree Hill, trying to read them like Braille. What had happened to the people who left these messages behind? What had they been trying to say?

Ms. K had told me that the hill held the stories of everyone who'd ever touched it.

"A story don't start where we tell it, you know..." She'd click her teeth as she parted my washed hair with her twisted fingers, and gently oiled my scalp. She'd comb the knots out of each wiry handful, holding the roots firmly to avoid yanking my head. "...is like a web, hard to unravel."

I wasn't sure if she meant the stories or my hair.

It didn't matter now anyway. I was miles away

from Ms. K, Samaan Bay, and everything I was trying to leave behind.

Suddenly, in the forest, a Jumbie Bird gave an echoing, weeping cry. A chill ran down my neck. Strange. Those small owl-like birds only came out at night. Da had told me that the call of a Jumbie Bird meant that someone was going to die.

I pulled my twists up into a bun, hands shaking. The sun was high in the sky. What time was it? I yanked out my phone and stared at the screen. Getting here had taken three hours! Twice as long as it had with Da. I shoved the phone back into my backpack and headed up the path that curved around the sides of the hill.

Heat glued my clothes to my skin. I'd forgotten how hard it was to get up this trail. The gravel path was narrow and steep, with no railing. I tried not to look down.

Finally, I made it to the top, panting and soaked with sweat. I stood on the edge of a large flat clearing, the size of two or three houses, covered in red dirt, stripped of all trees but one. At the furthest end was a large samaan tree, the Rain-Tree, shaped like a giant's open umbrella.

From up here, the view was insane. The hill

was in a valley full of multicoloured trees that stretched down to Samaan Bay. The bay gave way to the wide ocean, shimmering in blue-green and gold. Surrounding the valley was a mountain range, shaped like a horseshoe opening out to the sea. Those forested mountains were much taller than the dry, red hill on which I stood. They were like lush carpet piled up against the sky, in so many shades of green.

I walked to the side of the hill that looked away from the sea. Hidden somewhere in the mountain range beyond, were the abandoned buildings of the 'Zoo', completely overgrown by trees.

The Zoo didn't exactly match its name. For one, it wasn't an actual zoo. Da said that in the early 2000s, it was a research centre owned by an international company that had leased the land from the government. No one knew exactly what they used the facility for, except that it was top-secret and heavily guarded by foreign security.

People from the village claimed that animals of all kinds: chickens, pigs, cows, monkeys, manakins and mosquitoes, were experimented on there.

Animals, and, according to the rumours, "Humans too..."

The villagers had called the place the 'Zoo' and avoided it like the plague. Then, a few years ago, without explanation, the company just up and left. The Zoo was abandoned. To this day though, it was a place no one ever went; haunted by ghosts.

I had no intention of breaking that rule. There were other places to hide. Besides, I didn't know exactly where the Zoo was, other than 'in the mountains', and I certainly wasn't about to go looking for it.

Da had warned me about the Zoo when he brought me up here to Rain-Tree Hill, just before leaving for his new job in the U.S. We had spent the morning exploring the hill and the forest around it. From the moment I'd decided to run away, I knew that I'd come here first, before finding another place to lay low.

A crooked smile crept across my face. Once Da heard that I was missing, he'd be on the next flight to Trinidad. I'd give him three or four days to get the news that I was gone, fly down to the island from New York, and take the long drive out to Samaan Bay to join the search. Then I'd let the search party find me. I'd come out of hiding with some sob-story about being lost in the forest. Everyone would be so relieved. Then I'd talk to Da face-to-face, tell him again how unhappy I was; how serious I was about going to live with him.

A small voice inside pointed out that my plan was crazy. I told it to shut up and get with the programme. I had to do something drastic to get Da's attention. With the new baby, Mum barely had time to talk to me, far less really listen. As cute as Baby Tayo seemed, I called him "the Terror" for a reason. At this point, he pretty much held Mum hostage and nothing I told her was getting through.

Da kept saying to give it time, that Samaan Bay would be a great new adventure, but it was just another place where I was ignored.

"Send pictures," he told me, just before leaving to catch his flight, squeezing me in a bear hug that smelled like black coffee and mint, "it'll be like I was there."

It wasn't.

During our camping trips, Da had taught me everything I knew about surviving in the wild. Now, I would use it to bring him back to me.

My stomach whined. Time for lunch. I'd had one of the sandwiches and sports drinks in my backpack when I'd entered the forest, but that felt like years ago. The sun hammered down on my head. I was parched. There was no shade in the clearing other than the Rain-Tree. I walked over and sat under it with a sigh, sipping from one of the bottles of water in my bag. Ms. K had packed two large thermoses of water for me and two more for Jake. Plus, I had an extra can of the sports drink. So, I should be fine for the next few days on my own. Still, Da had taught me that it was always best to conserve water.

On a hot day like this, the Rain-Tree's shade was a lifesaver. All around me, its roots stretched out in different directions, like dolphins cresting the sea. I looked up at the web of branches above me, covered with hairy ferns, spiky bromeliads and what looked like large, hanging, wooden, bean pods.

This tree was a world of its own. Still, I knew I couldn't stay here forever. The net of leaves was shielding me from the sun right now, but at the slightest sign of rain the leaves would fold up on themselves and I would be soaked. Hence the name: 'Rain-Tree'.

I took one of the food containers out of my bag. Ms. K's bake and saltfish sandwiches tasted even better on the hill. I devoured one ravenously, crunching bits of sweet green pepper, licking salty drops of coconut oil off my fingers. She'd packed some for Jake too – half of them filled with saltfish and the rest with guava jam. I'd ration my meals over the next three days to make sure that I had enough.

Hopefully, no one would miss me until Jake came home that evening. A worrying thought slithered across my mind. What if Mum called Jake to see if I'd arrived safely at the smelter? It would kick the whole search process off early. Maybe I should leave the hill now and get to another, less obvious, hiding place.

I slid the food container back into my bag and stood up, holding a sandwich in my hand. I'd eat this one quickly and leave. The sun was high in the sky and there was no breeze. My clothes stuck to my skin. Mosquitoes whined in my ears. I waved them away. There was a long-sleeved shirt in my backpack, but it was too hot to wear now. The hum grew louder. Too many insects. Maybe I should put on that shirt after all. I jerked in pain and slapped my neck.

Something had stung me, again.

"Ouch!" I groaned.

It hurt much more than a mosquito bite.

In my palm was another gnat; its green light beeping out. What was this? Up close, the gnat looked metallic, like a tiny silver drone, with a green light flashing inside its head. Suddenly, I heard a whir.

I looked up. Above me, swirling around the trunk of the Rain-Tree, was a shining neon-green cloud, like fireflies. Except, fireflies didn't bite. My skin was being dotted with stings. I grabbed my backpack and turned to run, but the swarm spread quickly, filling the air around me. The hum rose to a buzz. I swatted my arms, trying to get to the path that led downhill.

In an instant, the lights were on me and with them a hundred tiny points of pain. The insects were all around me, flying into my clothes and face. I shielded my eyes with one hand and swung my other arm wildly, trying to keep away from the sides of the hill and the long drop to the ground below.

As the swarm spun around me, I fell to my knees. My skin was on fire. I scrambled to my feet and ran a short way forward, but they were on me again, peppering me with stings. This time I fell harder, flat on my face. I could do nothing but try and catch my breath. After a while, I noticed a change. None of the insects were biting me. But they weren't gone either. Their hum seemed to hover right over my back.

A picture popped into my head. It was of Mum, sitting next to her easel in the garden of our old house in Cascade, in the hills above the city of Port of Spain. My parents sold the house when they got divorced, but back then it was still our home.

There, in the garden, I could see Mum's face, calm and focused. She'd been working on a piece for her next exhibition, but now she was motionless in front of the wild, dark canvas, her orange head-tie as still as the rest of her body. I was seven then, standing next to her in the low grass.

"Mama," I whispered, "what you doing?"

She answered me through half-closed lips. "Being still."

Then she gently moved one finger and murmured, "Look..."

My eyes followed her hand. Then I saw it, zooming in and out of bright red bougainvillea flowers: an emerald-green hummingbird with royal purple wings, a shining turquoise back, and cobalt tail.

The tiny bird hung there in the air for a moment, its long narrow beak buried in the heart of a flower, wings moving so fast they seemed invisible. Then it was gone.

Now, years later, face down in the dirt on Rain-Tree Hill, I thought about that moment. I forced myself to be still. From the sound of it, the swarm was right above me. I could feel their whirring energy, hear their hum of rage. The hum rose to a roar. The pulse of sound pressed my body into the dirt. I felt something warm drip from my nose. The insects hung above me, waiting. Then slowly, the sound began to fade. After a while, I could picture the small green lights leaking away.

Finally, it was quiet.

I lay on my stomach, every inch of my body inflamed. There was no sound. I wanted to move, but what if they came back? After what felt like hours, I held my breath and rolled over on my left side. I bit my lip to keep from screaming in pain. As I turned, I heard a series of light pings, as though a set of nails had fallen from my body. Through my swollen eyelids, I could just make out tiny silver balls on the ground next to my face. Were they the curled-up bodies of dead insects, their green lights gone out? I didn't want to stick around to find out.

I tried to get up, but every movement was agony.

My head felt like it was made of lead. I fought to stand, but my body dragged me back down to the dirt. My eyes glazed over. Sleep slid up and took me away.

Chapter Four

RUN

In my dream, I was trapped at the dinner table while Jake cracked another one of his engineering jokes. Mum was giggling like a girl, her face all soft and round with the extra weight she'd gained from the baby. Meanwhile, Tayo the Terror wasn't living up to the name I'd given him. Instead, he was squealing with laughter, bald except for one puff of hair at the front of his head. His arms were swinging so high that I could see the birthmark shaped like a leafy stalk on his wrist, and the dimples that even I had to admit were kind of cute. He was cracking up because Mum and Jake were laughing, and that only made them laugh more.

Jake kept going. He leaned over to kiss my mum, all romantic movie star-like, announcing: "I'm Bond. Ionic bond. Taken, not shared."

"Okay Mr. Chemistry..." Mum grinned, rolling her eyes, but she kissed him back, looking ridiculously happy, as if everything around her was enough.

I just sat there thinking about Da and the old us, until I couldn't take it anymore.

I heard myself scream, "WHAT. IS. SO. FUNNY?"

I wasn't planning on being that loud, or hitting the table, or knocking over my glass.

As it broke, everything crashed into silence.

"Zo Adia Joseph!" Mum's usually warm voice had a cracked edge.

It's never good when they use your full name.

"Marie, it's okay," Jake looked back and forth between us, trying to keep the peace. "Come on Zo, let me help you clean up."

Tayo bawled as Mum rocked him in her arms.

She was staring at me with those wide-set, deep-brown eyes of hers that squinted when she was working on a new painting. She had the long, fan-like lashes that I'd always wanted, and the mole under her left eye that I had too - the black dot that she called "our beauty mark".

Those eyes used to make me feel like there was no one in the world that she loved as much as me, except maybe Da. Only this time, as I ran out of

34

the room, her eyes had the laughter knocked out of them. They were filled with pain that I'd caused, yet again.

I knew then that I had to go through with it. I had to leave.

****

"Time to get up!"

What? I groaned and shifted from my side to my back, trying to get comfortable on the hard bed. Trust Jake not to buy a good mattress. Everything ached.

"Wake up Miss Know-it-All!"

It was Ms. K's gravelly voice. Why was she in my room at this ungodly hour?

"Tired..." I muttered, without opening my eyes, "more sleep."

"Listen eh. You not getting me into any more trouble here today," Ms. K hissed.

"Ouch!" Something hard and bristly jabbed me in the stomach.

Was this woman poking me with a broom? I tried to open my eyes and couldn't. A golden light shone behind my closed eyelids.

"This is mind-mail, silly girl. You can only get them with your eyes closed. You think I could just come up here in person?"

Ms. K seemed highly irritated. I'd better get up. Wait... mind-mail? What was she talking about? I still couldn't open my eyes. A cold jolt of fear ran through me.

"Hurry up and listen," she hissed, "it takes energy to send these, and they can be tracked, so I don't have much time."

The light in my closed eyes grew stronger and came into focus. A massive golden spider leaned over me, pointing at me with one of its long, furry legs.

My brain hiccupped and stalled.

"Yes, Miss Wrong-and-Strong," the giant spider muttered in Ms. K's hoarse voice, staring at me with a thick serving of scorn, "you didn't want to listen. Now you better get up!"

I couldn't even scream. It all flooded back: her sudden change on the road near the smelter.

Ms. K is a spider! A giant spider... rang over and over in my head.

"Whaa... How? Don't eat me!"

How was I talking without moving my lips? Mind-mail, she'd called it. Okay, this was insane. I kept fighting to open my eyes.

"Child, please," Ms. K sucked her teeth scornfully. "I don't eat foolish people. Listen. Get up now and come home," her round eyes glinted strangely, "while you still can."

Then she was gone, leaving darkness behind.

I lay there for a while, before trying to open my eyes again. This time they lifted slowly and painfully. My eyelids were swollen. I could hardly move. Every part of my body hurt. I knew where I was now, and it wasn't in bed. I was stuck on Rain-Tree Hill, looking up into the black and silver sky. It was night-time. I had slept the entire day away. How was that possible?

The insects! I looked around carefully from my spot on the ground, barely turning my head. There was no sign of their green glowing lights. And no sign of Giant Spider Ms. K either.

My mind spun. None of this made any sense. Had I hit my head when I was running from the swarm?

Suddenly, drops of water fell on my body. The drops became tiny streams. Rain fell with a soft shhhh. It soothed my skin and eased my pain. Tears of relief burned my eyes. Soon, I was able to flex the muscles in my arms and legs. I listened. There was no hum or buzz, just the sound of wind and rain. I sat up slowly. Dark clouds moved out of the way, flooding the clearing with moonlight. What were those things that had attacked me? They were the weirdest biting insects I had ever seen. And what was Ms. K: a female Anansi the Spider?

I shook my head. That couldn't be it. I'd hit my skull, or there was something in the insects' stings – a chemical of some kind that had messed with my brain. Old Yancy's warning back at the market was starting to make sense. Either way, I needed to get out of here now.

My backpack lay next to me. There was a torch in it, and my phone. I'd call Mum and get her to send someone to end this nightmare and bring me home. Was the search party already out, or would they wait until daylight to come look for me?

My stomach flipped. By now, Mum must be worried sick. Coming here had been a huge mistake.

I staggered to my feet, scrambled for my bag, and pulled out my phone. How late was it? I had no idea. The phone's screen was blank. I pressed the 'ON' button. Nothing. The battery was dead. I swallowed the panic rising in my throat.

There, a couple of feet away, was one of my empty bottles and foil from the sandwich that had been in my hand. Out of habit, I walked over and picked them up. No point leaving rubbish on the hill. Suddenly, something swarmed my hand. I screamed, dropping everything. My hand was squirming with a life of its own. Shaking and slapping like crazy, I spun away from the tree. I was halfway across the clearing when it hit me. I looked more closely at my hand in the moonlight and dusted off the ants. My face burned. Silly. Thankfully, there was no one around to see me make a fool of myself. I walked back to the sandwich wrapper strewn in the dirt, covered with nothing but ants. My backpack was next to it, unbothered.

The rain stopped but the wind whipped past me. It was chilly up here at night. I pulled out a long-sleeved shirt and put it on over my cotton tee. Then I took my backpack, gave it a few hard shakes, and hung it over my shoulders.

Da had warned me many times against leaving food lying around in the forest. In hindsight, I was lucky it was just ants, and not even the biting kind. I breathed heavily and dusted my hands off one last time, trying to calm myself down. After all, this wasn't the Amazon. Yes, Trinidad was close to South America, but it was still an island, too small for big predators. Despite Ms. K's endless stories, jumbies didn't exist (at least, that's what I told myself), and there were no jaguars, bears, crocodiles, or wolves, like in other parts of the world. Anacondas were rare and stuck close to water, same as the gator-like caiman. The ocelot, a wild cat hunted to the point of extinction, was extremely hard to find.

Ants, I could handle. I knocked the empty bottle on the ground and threw it in the carrier bag in my backpack. I'd leave the rest of my sandwich to them.

A big yellow moon came out from behind the clouds. It shed a lot of light, but I turned on my torch anyway. If I stuck to the trail through the forest, I could make it home on my own. I left the Rain-Tree and walked to the far end of the hilltop, towards the track that curved down and around the rocky slope. I moved slowly, dislodging small pebbles as I went. It was steeper than I remembered. My foot slipped on loose stones. A few potentially broken bones later, I was at the bottom of the hill.

I hesitated, with my back against the still-warm rock, looking out at the silver clearing around the base of the hill, between me and the dark curve of forest. Maybe I should wait until morning. I thought about the path through the forest. Snakes were probably the biggest threat, especially poisonous ones like the diamond-backed mapepire or the red, black and white-striped coral. One bite from either of those snakes could be deadly.

It wasn't worth the risk. I could wait in the clearing until dawn. If no one came looking for me by then, I would find my way home in daylight. I looked again at the forest beyond the hill. It was a patchy mix of darkness and moonlight, full of strange shapes. Some of them looked like round, shining lights. Torches?

"Hey!" I called, then was still.

The lights began to move toward me. They were red and getting bigger. I stood there frozen, my torch dangling uselessly from one hand, as the red circles came close to the edge of the trees, a couple of metres away from me. It was then that I heard a low, rumbling noise and the sound of cracking branches. Those lights were eyes.

Crawling out of the trees at the far end of the clearing, was an animal from my worst nightmares. Even on all fours, it was my height, with the long head, body and tail of an alligator, but far larger than any I had ever seen. It had rows of sharp bony spikes running from its head to the tip of its swaying tail. Its six legs were short and bent on either side of a hanging belly. The claws on its feet were hooks. Teeth hung over the sides of its mouth - the razor-sharp jaws of a meat-eater. It stared at me through bright red eyes with long vertical slits. Yet the most shocking thing was the creature's skin.

It was as wet as a salamander's, completely white from nose to tip, except for the lines of green veins showing through. It was like a creature that had been skinned alive, revealing the slippery flesh underneath. Flesh-skinner, was all I could think, staring at its slick hide. It could probably skin me alive. I just stood there, frozen in place.

The beast bared its teeth, and the smell of old fish flew toward me on the wind. I gagged. It stared at me with sly eyes. I could swear it smiled.

Run.

I turned and sprinted in the opposite direction, past the hill, into the forest. Behind me, I could hear the scrabble of sliding dirt and stones, the crack and crash of trees. Hopefully, the undergrowth would slow it down. I held the torch in front of me, jumping over roots, and ducking under branches. I didn't dare look back. I could hear it somewhere behind me: a repeating snarl that started low then got louder and higher, until it was a scream that seemed almost human. I pushed myself to run faster, ignoring the knot in my side.

My backpack hooked on some bushes as I scrambled through them. It dragged me backwards. I tried to pull free. I could hear the Flesh-skinner getting closer. I could smell it: a thick swampy rotten-egg smell. I yanked myself forward, but the backpack wouldn't budge. It was me or this bag. I had to leave it behind. I squeezed out of it and kept running.

Sweat blinded me. My legs whipped past each other. I stumbled but kept going. Any second, that thing might reach out and grab me. The thought alone gave me wings. I dashed between the trees. Did I have time to swing myself up into their branches? What if it could climb? There was no time to stop and find out. I kept running. Trees rushed past me. The ground started rising, slowly at first, then more steeply. I gasped for air. I felt the beast fall back slightly, but it was still close. I forced myself to go even faster.

Just then, I heard Da shout, "Watch out!" in my head.

I picked up speed and burst through the trees into... nothing.

I clawed at the air. The thing behind me screamed. Too late. I slid down feet first.

I fell for a long time. Or at least, it felt that way.

I tried to stop myself with my hands and feet but could get no solid hold. All I managed to do was slow myself down, landing more gently than I'd expected. As soon as I hit the ground, I scrambled forwards on my hands and knees, expecting the Flesh-skinner to come sliding down after me.

Nothing happened.

I looked up. No sign of the beast.

I prayed that it was gone. In the moonlight, I could tell that I was at the bottom of a deep, narrow gorge. It was a miracle I hadn't broken any bones. My torch was smashed on the ground next to me. Now I had nothing but the moon to see by.

I stood up slowly. The ravine had high walls, topped by twisted trees that spread their arms up to the sky. I couldn't hear or smell the Flesh-skinner. The trees were still. Maybe it was up there, waiting quietly out of sight. Either way, it didn't seem willing to try these steep slopes.

That gave me some room to breathe, but not much. I looked left and right. The ravine turned a blind corner in both directions. I stayed as quiet as possible. God alone knew what else was down here with me. Clouds ate the moon. I crouched against the nearest wall in darkness, straining for any sign of movement.

Maybe if I made it to daylight, I would see a way out.

At least, for now, I was still alive.

Chapter Five
CATCH

I sat crouched at the bottom of the deep and narrow gorge, waiting for a sliver of daylight. I shivered as clouds kept trapping and releasing the moon, moving everything in and out of darkness.

My mind drifted back to the night before I ran away. Jake had been trying to convince me, as usual, about the joys of Samaan Bay.

"Take the Independence Festival," he'd announced.

"I'd rather not," I muttered.

"One whole week at the end of August..."

He went on and on about how it showed off the many cultures that made our island unique. But all I heard was one thing.

"The end of August!" I stared at him in shock. "That's weeks from now!"

What did he expect me to do for the rest of the holidays?

Mum glanced up from feeding the baby and shot me a warning look.

Even with her hair sticking up in every direction and half-moon shadows under her eyes, Marie Joseph (Lee now, since marrying Jake) was beautiful in a don't-mess-with-me kind of way. Her skin was dark and shining under the stained-glass lamps of the cottage Jake had rented for us, outside of the village.

Her face said, Zo, please don't.

I tried to take some deep breaths.

Jake carved his food with giant, chemical-stained hands. He kept going on about how everyone from the surrounding villages, and anyone who had ever left Samaan Bay, came back for the celebrations.

"There's probably a reason they left in the first place," I mumbled under my breath.

I, for one, had just got here and was more than ready to leave. A few days of fun at the end of August couldn't fix this mess. But Jake kept talking as if he couldn't see the sour look on my face.

Last year, he declared, was his first time here. The night before the festival, people had taken over the streets with exploding fireworks. They burst bamboo rods open, twisted them into fantastical shapes, then lined them with clay-pot deyas, filled with coconut oil and floating wicks that lit up the night.

The next day, men, women and children coated in mud, paint and abeer, streamed into the village, beating loud djembe and tassa drums. Bands filled the air with the rhythmic melodies of steelpan, while towering Moko Jumbie stilt-walkers guarded the streets.

Dragon and lion dancers in winding costumes with piercing eyes and ferocious smiles, stunned the crowd with their acrobatic leaps and turns.

Then Midnight Robbers took over the square, wearing wide-brimmed black hats lined with swinging fringe, topped with skulls and other dread designs. White powder masked their faces. Piercing whistles kept the crowd spellbound. Their black satin capes bore skeletal silver shapes that spun around them as they turned. In slyly comic and threatening 'Robber Talk', they boasted of their origins and exploits. They invented speeches inspired by legends like the Epic of Sundiata, Nanny of the Maroons, rebel leader Hyarima, and more.

Kathak and Odissi dancers, in striking make-up and bejewelled clothes, told ancient stories with rhythmic movements of their faces, hands and feet, to the beat of tabla drums and the shaking sounds of the brass ghungroo bells around their ankles.

Giggling children ran everywhere, stuffing handfuls of halwa rich with raisins and nuts, slices of shiny plait bread topped with smoked herring and picked cucumbers, crispy sticks of fried kurma, sada roti lined with roasted garlic and tomato choka, seasoned accra fishcakes, meat-filled cornmeal pastelles, jaw-breaking caramel and sesame-seed benne balls, fruity black cake, hot corn soup cooked with aromatic herbs, and finely-ground cassava farine, into their wide-open mouths.

I had to admit; that didn't sound so bad.

"And this year we'll be here for it - up close and personal!" Jake kept saying, looking for a hint of excitement on my face.

I refused to crack.

"That's interesting, right Zo?" Mum chimed in, but the small 'v' on her forehead said that she, too, was doubtful about this vision of us dancing through the streets at all hours of the day and night.

"Hmm," was all I let myself say.

I knew from Da that this version of Trinidad and Tobago's history as one giant party was far from the truth.

The question I really wanted to ask was, exactly how did Mr. 'Great Expectations' Jake plan for us to do all this celebrating with Tayo the Terror around, crying and needing everyone's attention?

In any case, most of the things Jake talked about, I could see back home in the city: not all together, sure, but at different times of the year, from Christmas to Carnival, Diwali, Chinese New Year, Emancipation Day, or Eid ul Fitr. Or I could go to the next-door island of Tobago with its own history, culture, and beaches where I could actually swim.

To make a bad thing worse, Mum had suggested that after the holidays, we might spend the next school term here, while Jake finished getting Samaan's Bay's new smelter up and running.

No way. I was done being stuck. I had a plan. I was going to run away.

Now I sat trapped in the dark belly of a gorge, jumping at every sound and shadow around me. Was the Flesh-skinner or some other twisted creature coming back to finish me off?

Either way, nothing was going according to plan.

What I wouldn't give to be part of that Samaan Bay festival now – to eat some of that mouth-watering food and most of all, to see my Mum and Da again.

****

Just when I was about to lose it, morning came. I hadn't slept a wink. My eyes were dry and my mouth felt sandy, as if I'd trekked through the desert all night. Questions crowded my mind. What on earth was that thing that had chased me? How come it was here in the forest, without so much as a whisper to warn of its existence?

Speaking of warning, the village should be out looking for me by now. My family were probably scouring the forest. I stiffened. That beast would hunt the search party too. My heart thumped. I strained my ears for any sound. Maybe I would hear them in the trees above, calling my name. That might give me enough time to scream a warning.

I stared around me in the daylight. I was sprawled on a pile of small stones. White pebbles of various sizes lined the dirt floor. As I got up, they cracked and crunched beneath my feet. I bent over to tie my shoelaces and pulled back with a stifled scream. The pebbles weren't stones. They were the tiny skulls of creatures I didn't recognize, with delicate curved horns. I looked from side to side, my skin prickling. I was in a gorge littered with small, bleached bones.

I tried to scramble up the slope behind me, desperately hoping that the Flesh-skinner was long gone. But the gravel slipped under my feet and hands, dragging me down and making way too much noise. I had to be quiet.

What creatures' bones were under my feet? Their skulls were the size of coins. They seemed too small to be the Flesh-skinner's prey, but whatever had killed them had done a thorough job.

I looked around for a way out. On one side, the rock face was sheer and smooth. The side I'd come down was littered with steep dirt and gravel slopes, too unsteady to bear my weight. I fumbled at my side. My cutlass was in its sheath, still hooked to my belt. At least I had this. Da always said to never go into the forest without a blade. Thinking about him comforted me. What would he say now? Stay low, keep moving. Keep your eyes peeled. I pulled the cutlass out by its wooden handle. Sunlight glinted on the sharp metal edge. At least now I could defend myself, or try to. I straightened my back, bit my lip, and forced my feet to move.

I peeked around the corner to my left and saw that the ravine narrowed to an opening that was too small for me to fit through. Time to try the other side... I moved quietly to my right, toward the other bend in the ravine, trying not to crunch the bones under my feet. Thinking about what might have left them there sucked the strength out of my legs, but I made myself keep walking.

"Courage is the foundation of all the virtues," Da would say in his warm, bass voice, quoting Dr. Maya Angelou.

Then Mum would chime in with her favourite verse: "There is no fear in love..."

"Easier said than done guys," I whispered.

I was the one trapped in this crazy place.

Still, I repeated their words to myself, and they helped me put one foot in front of the other.

Carefully, I looked around the bend. Ahead of me was a long stretch of gorge that went on for several feet before it curved around yet another corner. My heart pumped hard in my chest. The walls in this section of the ravine looked more jagged, with rough outcrops of rock. Maybe here I would have better luck climbing out.

I slipped the cutlass back into its sheath and tried pulling myself up the wall. It didn't work. My legs were shaking, and the rock was slippery. I kept sliding back down. I sank to the ground, defeated. It was no use. I had no choice but to wait for someone to come find me. I thought about the search party looking for me with that creature on the loose. Without someone to warn them, they didn't stand a chance. I couldn't stop my hot, silent sobs.

Wait, what was that? A rumbling noise like a distant landslide. I jumped to my feet. Was the Flesh-skinner finally crawling into the gorge? I tried again to claw my way out but kept sliding right back down. The noise grew louder. It was getting closer. I dashed from wall to wall, looking for a place to grab hold. The noise stopped. Hopefully, whatever it was, it had gone another way. I was still trying to get a grip on the rock when a large brown ball sped around the corner.

Before I could move, the rolling mass broke into a flood, skittering over the floor and walls toward me. I turned to run, but it was too late. They were all over me, tens of big, furry spiders, jumping over my legs, arms, face and hair. They covered my mouth so I couldn't scream and tied my hands, feet and waist with sticky webs. Together, the spiders tugged at me and the webs, as if with one mind.

Now I knew what had left those bones behind.

I struggled, trying to break free. I couldn't let them drag me away to their nest and eat me, but the webs were as strong as ropes. Every second, more webs wrapped around me. I gathered my strength for one last fight, when I realised that the spiders weren't dragging me deeper into the gorge. They were pulling me out of it.

I hesitated and in those few seconds the trap was complete. I was wrapped in webs from the shoulders down, with a sticky piece of webbing over my mouth, being hoisted up the side of the ravine.

I heard a tired voice groan, "Man, this girl is heavyyy."

"Ent they all?" someone drawled back.

The spiders were talking. After the metallic gnats and a ravenous beast, I shouldn't have been surprised.

A skinny spider with a high-pitched voice and green bandana over its head piped up. "How many of these Two-Legs we got to rescue today? My back hurts!"

A chorus of different voices snapped: "How we supposed to know? We following orders, same as you!"

"Okay, okay," a spider with a red jumbie-bead necklace advised, "no need to bite Yemi's head off. This ent her fault."

"Bite her head off? I doh eat junk food!" laughed an elegant, long-legged spider, jangling the blue bangles on its legs.

"Ha, very funny Adita," another one snorted, under its tiny, wide-brimmed cricket hat.

"Less talking, more working!" a plump, glossy spider ordered.

"But who die and make you the boss?" a skinny one snapped.

The bossy spider bristled. "Listen. Don't test me eh! I am not your mother. And Gopaul luck is not Seepaul luck."

"But who is Seepaul?" a clueless spider chimed in.

"If you would spend more time building your webs instead of prancing all over the blessed forest, you would..."

"Um, excuse me," a spider with four pairs of spectacles (yes, spectacles!) over its eight eyes, interrupted, "Could we just focus please? I left

Amba watching the children and you know how she is."

"Alright, alright, is true. You know them children have no behaviour!"

Hoarse laughter filled the air.

After more of this bickering, and some tugging and pulling, I was out of the gorge. I lay there, stunned.

Two scruffy spiders near my head went back and forth, "What we waiting on? Our orders was to get her out of there, right?"

"Shhh. You talk too much!"

"Says who?"

"Says me, of course!"

"I thought you said not to talk."

The spiders scrambled all over me as if checking and reinforcing their webs. Where were they going to drag me next? My cutlass was still in its sheath at my side, pressed against my body by webs. If I could just get to it... I tried to squirm and wiggle my fingers, but I could barely move.

"Hey!" the spiders scattered off me in protest. "They ent paying us enough for this!"

"You stay still Little Missie," a massive spider murmured on my left. It crawled up onto my webbed arm. This one was the biggest of the bunch, four times the size of my hand, with a red striped scarf on its head, a thick hairy body, and long bristly legs. My skin tingled, itching to slap it off me, but I couldn't move an inch.

My heart jumped in my chest. As if talking spiders weren't enough, this one was different from the others. It had a mechanical leg made of silver metal, complete with gears and joints, with pincers on the end of it like a crab. I stared, blinked, and stared again. The leg was still there. The spider moved up my side to my shoulder, whirring and creaking all the way. I could see now that one of its eyes was red and shining like an electric light. It clicked in and out of its head on the end of what looked like a tiny telescope. The spider's other eyes were scarred, sightless – two of them covered by an eye patch. What madness was this? I wriggled and tried to scream, but my mouth and body were wrapped in webs like an unfinished Egyptian mummy.

"Calm down, girlie," the spider ordered, in no way calming me down, "you never seen a robotic arm? Or is it me pretty eye got you shaking in your boots?"

The others laughed. I had to be dreaming. This spider sounded like an old pirate-woman who had sailed the wild and restless sea. I blinked hard, trying to wake myself up, but it was still there.

"We gotta get going Cap'n Peg," one of the spider-crew murmured respectfully. It was wearing a pink beret covered in medals.

There was a chorus of "Mm-hms and yes-es" all around.

"Stay busy and mind your manners, ye scurvy landlubbers!" the spider with the metal leg growled.

Who talked like that? And where were they taking me next? I squirmed hard, trying to get out.

The other spiders mumbled and complained, but they hurried to obey, checking the webs that held me tight.

Cap'n Peg nestled in the twists of my hair, scanning the forest and sky as if on the lookout for something or someone.

I jumped when she whispered in my ear: "The Boss says to follow the river and don't trust people you don't know. This is the last message she can send you, y'hear?"

"Urgh-mmm-urgh?" I stared at her wildly.

She rolled her one good eye.

"Child," she sighed softly, "stick break in your ears?"

The fur on her legs tickled my face horribly. I tried not to move or breathe.

"Say nothing about this," she went on, "as you love your life. Remember, those who can't hear, will feel!"

She stared me down with her laser-beam eye. I nodded. Then she reached her metal pincer toward my face and yanked the webbing from my mouth.

In that second, the spiders sliced the webs covering my body, cutting me loose. I was free.

I sat up slowly and opened my mouth, to ask what on earth was going on.

"Shh!" Cap'n Peg hissed right in my face.

I scrambled back with a stifled scream. She held on to my hair like a sailor swinging from the mast of a ship. The other spiders scampered to a safe distance, quarreling. "Crazy Two-Legs!"

"Not. A. Word… If you know what's good for you," Cap'n Peg muttered softly.

I noticed then that she had a cowrie shell bracelet around one of her non-metal legs. She grinned at me suddenly. I didn't know spiders could grin, but then, they weren't supposed to talk and wear jewellery either.

Without another word, she flipped out of my hair and sped away. Like a unit, the other spiders followed, jumping out of sight over the edge of the ravine.

I sat there, dazed and sweaty, surrounded by bits of webbing, trying to make sense of it all.

The 'Boss' Cap'n Peg had referred to, must be Ms. Kofi. She was the only giant spider-person I knew. As for the advice about following the river – I was lost out here. How was I supposed to find a river in the middle of the forest? And about not trusting people I didn't know... I was all alone in this place. There was no one left to trust.

Where had these creatures come from and how had no one in the village even mentioned their existence? In my head, I kept seeing Cap'n Peg, the spider with the mechanical leg, telescope eye, and urgent warning. Mechanical. Metal. My mind leaped back to the gnats that had stung me on Rain-Tree Hill. They had looked like tiny drones up-close. I could still hear the pings as the ones I slapped fell to the ground. Maybe they were drones. Forged. Made. I felt dizzy with what that would mean.

Someone had done this – made these creatures what they were.

The Zoo! They had experimented on animals years ago. Who knew what they'd made? Maybe some of those animals had escaped and survived in the forest until now, but how come no one else had seen them?

A horrible possibility crawled into my mind. Maybe the people who had gone missing in the forest hadn't just gotten lost. Now that I thought about it, Ms. K had mentioned the occasional hunter and hiker who'd had "accidents" in the forest and vanished without a trace, in the years since the Zoo had closed. I thought that they were just stories, meant to keep me from going too far into the trees on my own. But now I knew the truth. Other people might have met creatures like this in the forest, but they hadn't lived to tell the tale. Instead, they were just the lonely and unlucky souls who had never made it back home.

Now, I could be one of them.

I stood up and tried to steady myself on my feet. Fear, exhaustion, and hunger made me weak. I thought of my backpack with horror, stuck on a bush somewhere. I'd lost everything: my supplies, food and water. I stumbled under the shade of a nearby Crappo tree. All I had left was my cutlass.

Wait. My long, stained cargo pants had a bunch of pockets. I checked them all and relief washed over me. I pulled out a flattened, melted, bar of chocolate in a sealed bag. It was better than nothing. I devoured a quarter of it. As I did, rain fell suddenly and heavily. I picked up a waxy leaf from the ground and curled it to my lips the way Da had taught me. I swallowed the trickle of rainwater that ran into my mouth, trying not to cry as I thought of him. I had to get out of here, to see him again.

I climbed a tree with branches low enough for me to reach, but all I could see were hills and forest in every direction. Perhaps in the mad dash from the Flesh-skinner, I had run somewhere into the mountain range around Rain-Tree Hill.

The gorge curved in both directions as far as my eyes could see. The spiders had pulled me up on the other side from where I'd fallen in. I couldn't think of any way to cross back over, or even spot where I'd come from in the first place. Now I was surrounded by steep slopes and deep ravines, out of sight of Rain-Tree Hill, the village, or the sea.

I wracked my brain, trying to think of a way out.

As I forced myself to calm down, the rain got me thinking. What if the gorge was no more than an old, usually dry riverbed? Now with the rain, maybe there was some water running down it. All rivers ran to the sea. If I walked on the side of the gorge in the direction of the rainwater, sooner or later I would come to the coast. From there, I could find Samaan Bay or some other village.

The spider had said, "Follow the river."

Maybe she was right. It was time to get going.

I inched to the edge of the ravine and looked down carefully through the rain. There was no sign of the spiders, just the water beginning to run in a thin stream at the bottom of the gorge, toward my left. That was the way to go.

I walked for hours along the bank of the ravine. As time passed, its sloping sides grew more and more shallow, until the once-steep gorge was nothing but a flat, dry bed of stones. The channel formed an S-like road of sorts, curving through the forest. It was an old riverbed, just as I'd suspected. My heart lifted a little. I might be home before nightfall.

To my right, shimmering green and gold batimamselles, dragonflies, chased in each other in a zigzag pattern only they understood. Their glittering, translucent wings reflected the light, as they skimmed through the air, ducked, hovered and sped like fairy racehorses above the dry channel.

On the riverbed itself, smooth, flat black stones with rounded edges, glistened in the sunlight. Every so often, I noticed seven or more stones arranged in an odd tower. Sometimes, strangely, the smallest stone was at the base of the tower. This stone seemed way too small to hold the larger ones balanced above it. Yet, miraculously, it did.

Even as I admired the beauty of the old channel, I couldn't afford to relax. I had to survive the Flesh-skinner and whatever else was out there. My senses were on high alert, tuned in to every sound and smell. This time, the Flesh-skinner wouldn't catch me by surprise. Once I heard it coming, I'd climb up onto the highest branch I could find. In the meantime, I moved as quietly as I could, keeping to the side of the dry riverbed, under the cover of trees.

Finally, I heard rushing water in the distance. It was coming from the forest up ahead. Had I made it to the sea?

I ran forward next to the rocky channel, bobbing and weaving through the trees. After a while, I had to slow to a walk. Then, I pulled up short.

"No!" My heart sank.

A powerful river blocked my path. The channel I'd followed had been nothing more than a dried-up tributary. The main river swirled in front of me, running from left to right, surrounded by forest. It looked too fast and deep to cross. I squeezed my nails into my palms, trying to stay calm. The logic still held. If I followed this large river downstream, I would get to the coast and eventually, closer to help. All this meant was that I had further to go.

I was tired, hungry, and thirsty. Now at least one of those problems could be solved. At a small pool springing off from the river, I knelt and drank my fill. I washed my face, arms, and neck quickly, keeping an eye out for movement around me. Then I kept going, walking in the same direction as the flow of the river. I slipped through the trees on the riverbank like a ghost, staying within sight of the water.

Suddenly, a sharp pain stabbed my stomach. Hopefully, it wasn't the water I just drank from the river. An image of squirming parasites flashed through my head. A loud belch burst from my mouth. Oh. Quenching my thirst had only made me hungrier and this was my stomach's way of protesting.

I couldn't help picturing a macaroni pie, baked to perfection, with a crisp crust and cheesy centre, melting next to pigeon peas cooked in creamy coconut milk, washed down with fresh-squeezed lime juice sweetened with honey. Of course, a meal like that wasn't complete without chicken, cut up and seasoned with garlic and fragrant herbs like chadon beni and chive, then browned in melted sugar, before being stewed to perfection with tomatoes, carrots, pimentos, and a hint of Scotch bonnet pepper.

My mouth watered. I took the small bag of chocolate from my pocket and forced myself to eat only half of what was left. There was no time to search for food. I needed to get downstream before nightfall. Without stopping, I might make it to the coast before sunset and not have to spend another night in the forest.

It hit me again how much I needed to see my parents. At this point, even Jake and the Terror would be a welcome sight.

"Help!"

The shout stopped me in my tracks. Was I hearing things?

"Help!"

No. It had come from the river.

I rushed to the edge of the current and leaned out of the trees, holding on to one of the trunks for safety. I looked right, then left, careful not to slip on the muddy bank. There, upstream, in the rushing river, was a head and splashing arms.

Someone was fighting to stay above water.

Chapter Six

SINK

"Over here!" I screamed.

The boy tried to paddle weakly towards the bank where I was standing, but the current dragged him away and he went under.

I scanned the river, desperate for any sign of life. His head burst from the water in the middle of the current.

"Hold on!" I shouted, spinning around.

There was a long branch on the ground. I hauled it towards me and threw myself down onto the bank. I locked my legs around a tree trunk and reached the branch across the water, as far as it could go.

"Grab this!" I yelled.

He swam toward me, but the current kept pulling him back.

"Come on," I begged, anchoring the branch under my chest, and gripping it with both hands.

The boy fought hard. He was so close. His right hand clutched the branch, then was ripped away. The force of the water was too strong. I could see the desperation in his eyes as he was sucked under for what must have felt like the hundredth time.

I tore off my boots and socks, then stopped. Even though I'd done years of competitive swimming, Mum had always warned me against getting into live water alone.

"Only swimmers drown," she'd caution me and my friends, reminding us about riptides and undertow.

I stared at this boy in the grip of the current, struggling to keep his nose above water. There was no time left. Diving in headfirst was a bad idea, so I waded in as fast as I could, then took a deep breath and glided forward hands-first. The force of the water was a shock. It was bitterly cold. I tried to stay calm and let the river take me. Constantly fighting the current would leave me with no strength left to save the boy.

The tumbling water kept pulling me under and soon, I needed to breathe. I kicked hard, trying to come up for air. Just when my lungs felt like they were about to explode, I got my face above water. I took a quick breath and swung my head around. There he was, not too far from me: a limp floating mass.

I grabbed him, turned him over on his back and moved behind him. With one arm across his chest, I pulled and kicked, trying to make it to the nearest bank. It took all my strength just to move a few inches. Then the current pulled us back toward the heart of the river.

I fought to breathe. It was no use. We were getting nowhere. For all I knew the boy in my grip had already drowned. Soon I would too. His weight bore me down. I gasped for air and swallowed a mouthful of water that tasted like metal. I thought of letting him go, trying to make it to the bank alone. Da's voice filled my head.

Before my gymnastics and swimming tournaments, wherever in the world he was, he would call to say, "Remember Zo, your best is enough."

I kicked hard, fighting to keep the boy's mouth and nose above the swelling water. My best... That was all I could do.

The current spun us around a bend, and I saw a thicket of bamboo. The sturdy green and yellow rods towered from a mudflat on the right side of the channel. Several long sticks of bamboo had fallen into the water. They were wedged in a makeshift barrier across that part of the river. I kicked hard, reached out and wrapped my arm around one of the ridged bamboo poles. The river rushed around us, but I held on.

Then, inch by inch, I pulled us along the length of bamboo toward the shallows. Once my feet could touch the bottom, I grabbed the boy under both arms and pulled him up onto the mudflat. My limbs were heavy and every muscle in my body was on fire, but there was no time to rest. I knelt at his side and put my ear next to his mouth and nose. No warm puff of air. Nothing.

I put both hands on his chest and pushed down firmly, trying to remember CPR.

"One, two, three, four, five, six..." I counted the compressions under my breath, two per second, letting his chest rise completely between pushes.

I checked his breathing again. Still nothing. My heart thumped. Everything swayed around me. I tilted his head back slightly, lifting his chin and opening his mouth. With the fingers of my right hand, I pinched his nose, breathed in deeply and covered his mouth with mine. Then I blew air into his mouth twice, watching his chest rise slightly each time. I kept the chest compressions going up to thirty counts, followed by two more breaths.

Still nothing.

"Come on!"

I repeated the cycle of thirty compressions and two breaths, more quickly this time. My heart pounded as I counted out loud and prayed that I was doing them the right way. Once he started breathing, I could stop. Why wasn't he breathing?

****

Suddenly, I was staring into the face of a beautiful woman. She was laughing, teeth white against her dark brown skin, and she was bald.

"Ma, can you pass the juice?" I felt my lips say, but the voice wasn't mine and that woman was not my mother.

Yet somehow, part of me felt at ease, like I knew her. The other part of me was freaking out. Where was I and how had I gotten here? Who were these people and where was the boy I'd just pulled from the river? He wasn't breathing. If I didn't get back to him soon, he would die.

"Here love," the woman handed me a thermos with a huge smile.

I reached out to take it with a tanned arm. A sense of horror spread over me. That wasn't my arm. The life vest, blue t-shirt and orange swim trunks I was wearing weren't mine either. I was in someone else's body – a boy's! But that was impossible.

I felt like I was spinning out of control, but the body I was in didn't seem to notice. I found myself taking a sip of cold juice from the thermos and running one hand over my head, feeling nothing but smooth skin. I was bald too. I felt the cool breeze on my head, arms and legs, and I loved it. Or at least, the boy loved it. I was hyperventilating, unnoticed, inside.

I tried to open my lips to say, "Who are you?" but nothing came out.

I was trapped in this body, able to do what it was doing and nothing more. What was even weirder, was that I could sense what the boy was feeling, but I was still myself, Zo, with all my own thoughts, feelings, and awareness of who I really was.

The difference was intense. The boy felt relaxed, totally unaware of my presence, while I screamed to get out.

The air around us was salty with sea spray. We were skidding over the ocean in a wooden boat, leaving white foam in our wake. It felt like flying, but I couldn't enjoy it. I kept trying to figure out what was happening and how.

The boat's motor roared over the bumpy waves. I turned to see a muscular man seated at the back, gently adjusting the tiller. He had no hair either. His head was cream-colored and smooth, shining under the sun's rays.

Wait. A boat with three bald people, South Asian background, two parents and a child. The family who'd gone missing! It didn't make sense, but somehow, I was with them - the family that everyone thought had drowned at sea.

The boy from the river: he must be their son! As impossible as it seemed, I was inside one of his memories.

According to the Samaan Bay villagers, only the family's overturned boat had been found. How had they all ended up in the water?

I tried shouting to the man and woman to watch

out, slow down, but my lips wouldn't open. I couldn't get this body to feel my sense of urgency, or even my presence, far less do or say anything I wanted.

I looked down. The boy's legs were long and tanned, his feet snug in blue and silver swim shoes. He was at peace, taking in the view, even as I yelled in silence. The boat sped around a tree-covered peninsula like an arm reaching out into the sea. That must be Hideaway Point. On the other side was a curve of golden beach, watched over by dense forest.

"One year!" the man handling the motor shouted happily, raising a bright pink paper cup high in the air.

I felt the boy grin from one adult to the other.

I was confused. One year of what?

The woman he'd called Ma was crying a little, or maybe it was the sea-spray in her eyes. Wait, no. I was shocked to feel tears spring up under the boy's eyelids as well, even as he laughed. His body was flooded with relief. His mother's smile was like the sun after a storm. My heart was bursting with a mix of emotions I couldn't control or understand.

Ma dashed the tears from her face.

"It's okay," she said, "we're here."

Where? I wondered. They were still a good way from the beach.

Without warning, the boat was slammed hard. It flew up in the air and flipped over, as though tossed by some massive invisible hand. The boy hit the water so hard it hurt. No one heard me scream. He sank into the seething waves, and I sank with him, trapped in his terror and my own.

****

I opened my eyes and took a jagged breath. I was out of the boy's memory, sucking in air.

How long had it lasted? Clearly not very long. I was still kneeling on the mudflat by the river, surrounded by bamboo. The boy lay in front of me, eyes wide and staring. I yanked my hands away. They burned with an invisible force. The vision had taken over like a light switch, flicking on at his touch. A hallucination? It had seemed so real. I'd been a prisoner in his mind, forced to live a moment in his life like it was my own. Now I crawled away from his wheezing chest, afraid to touch him, to be sucked back into memories that weren't mine.

The boy coughed and spluttered next to me. The CPR had worked. He was alive. I felt my stomach churn as he hacked up water and bile. I kneeled next to him with my hands clenched. My skin was inky next to his copper arms. I wanted to help him, but what had just happened? I slid further away on the mud, watching him like a hawk.

Even though his clothes were torn and covered in grime, I recognized his aqua t-shirt, orange swim-trunks and those blue and silver shoes. His hair was stubbly and uneven, but it was definitely him: the boy from the boat, the one who'd gone missing. Now he stared up at me weakly from the mudflat at the side of the river, wheezing and shivering like a reed.

Had I really entered his memory and if so, how? How had I come back?

I felt like I was going crazy, but there was no denying what I'd seen and felt. Something had hit the boat so hard... I shuddered, wondering if the Flesh-skinner could swim.

The boy sat up on the mudflat slowly, dripping and trembling. I jumped to my feet. He was taller than I was: thin and bony where I was round and strong. He stared at me like I was a ghost. I shivered too, suddenly cold. His eyes had seemed black at first, but now they were warm and brown. He had his father's eyes, but everything else came from his mum. There were the same thick eyelashes and sharp cheekbones, the same hooked nose and unruly eyebrows.

"Who...where?" he croaked.

"I'm Zo," I replied, my voice shaking, "you okay?"

He clearly wasn't.

To tell the truth, neither was I.

Chapter Seven
SEARCH

"Adri," I repeated the name the boy had told me, making sure to stay well out of his reach.

River water still tasted like metal on my tongue. My stomach rolled, but I kept my eyes glued on him. My arms and legs burned. Suspicion fought my relief at seeing another human.

Where had he come from in this crazy forest and what had just happened when I did CPR? It was like I'd fallen right into one of his memories. My brain buzzed as I tried to make sense of it.

Adri scrambled to his feet, staring at me wildly. I jumped back. If he knew that I'd been in his memory, no wonder he was terrified. I was too.

"My parents...! Where are they?" he croaked accusingly, his voice hoarse from coughing up water.

"How should I know?" I slung back. "You tell me!"

He crumpled, head in his hands. It all came rushing out. The last thing he remembered was being with his parents, on a boat at sea. Then he'd woken up, half-drowned in the tree-lined river, fighting for air. What had happened in between, he didn't know.

He seemed to have no clue that I'd been in his memory – no idea what I'd seen. I opened my mouth to tell him, then snapped it shut. The spider's warning from Ms. K had been not to trust anyone I didn't know. And I certainly didn't know this kid.

"Right," I raised my eyebrows at him, taking another step back, "no memory."

How had he gotten from the sea to the middle of the forest?

"Your family's been missing for three weeks," I threw out. "Everyone in Samaan Bay's been looking for you."

"Three weeks...!" Denial and shock crawled across his face.

His head sank.

I stared at him, dropping my fists. He shook, as the horror hit him in waves. I felt sick. Unless he was one of the best actors I'd ever seen, he was telling the truth.

"I'm so sorry," I whispered.

I'd been taking the word of a talking spider over another human, like that made sense. None of this did. I looked at Adri's shell-shocked face. Should I tell him about what I'd seen in his head? It might jolt his memory... or send him over the edge. Maybe he would think I was crazy. I was beginning to wonder myself.

A million questions raced through my mind. Clearly Adri had made it to shore after the boat overturned. Why had he come further inland, instead of waiting at the beach for someone to find him? Had he survived in the forest this long on his own? Unlikely. Maybe one or both of his parents had been with him. Where were they now? Perhaps the same thing that had separated him from them, had made him lose his memory.

I'd heard of people losing parts of their memory after hitting their heads, or some other terrible experience. I thought of all the creatures I'd met in the forest so far. Maybe Adri and his family had faced worse.

"Wh-what, who...?" Adri stuttered from his seat in the mud.

"I'm lost," I said slowly, "same as you."

That seemed obvious, but I didn't know what else to say. I thought of all the weird things that had happened since I'd seen Ms. K turn into a spider. Now I had a kid with amnesia to add to the list.

"Hey," I murmured as gently as I could.

Adri just sat there, clutching his head like he was trying to hold it in place. The sun beat down on the mudflat, shining on us and the bamboo, drying the wet clothes on our backs.

I looked up at the sky. What time was it?

"We have to get going," I told Adri in my most grown-up voice.

He looked up. His eyes were haunted, stamped with dark circles.

I told him about my plan to follow the river back down to the coast.

"It's the best way to reach someone, anyone, who can find your parents."

That seemed to sink in. His eyes focused on me slowly.

"Okay," he whispered.

"Here," I handed him the last of my chocolate.

He scarfed it down and looked at me for more.

"That's it, sorry."

Why was I apologizing? It wasn't like I had a restaurant in my back pocket.

"No... Thank you," he offered, still shaking.

I took a deep drink from the river and suggested he do the same. Maybe he'd been trying to get some water earlier when he tumbled in.

"Stay here," I ordered and before he could react, I rushed back for my socks and boots, shaking them out to make sure that nothing had crawled inside. When I got back, he hadn't moved an inch. He was still staring down at the mud.

"Come on," I said, trying to sound like I knew what I was doing.

He crawled to his feet.

"Hold on, wait." Something had fallen out of his pocket. I bent to pick it up and froze.

"Where'd you get this?" I asked numbly.

He looked confused.

The thing I'd picked up was a broken plastic key card, scraped and smeared with dirt. I could just make out the letters: Globa...Researc...entre.

The abandoned research centre. The Zoo. Adri had an old door key from the Zoo.

I backed away from him. "What were you doing at the Zoo?"

"What?" He stared at me like he had no idea what I meant.

"Don't play games with me," I warned him, trying to sound braver than I felt.

My heart slammed in my ears as I thought about all the creatures that had chased me so far, and the place that I thought they'd all come from.

"Adri, what were you doing there?"

He took a step toward me then stopped, arms dangling at his sides.

"What zoo?" His eyes were wide and helpless.

"I...I don't remember..."

"Don't lie to me!" I roared.

He stumbled backward, nearly falling into the river.

"I swear I don't know..."

I tried to calm down and think. Despite the sun, I was still soaked with water and sweat. The sun. How many hours of daylight did we have left? Maybe this kid had lost his memory since the accident, or maybe not. Maybe he had found his way to the Zoo or been dragged there. I took in his torn and filthy clothing, his wild and terrified eyes. He certainly looked like someone on the run. Either way, right now, what was out there in the forest was more of a threat to me than he was. I either had to leave him here or take him with me and move on.

"Okay, listen..."

I told him my dad's warnings about the Zoo, that I'd barely escaped some wild beasts in the forest and that my guess was that they came from the abandoned centre.

I didn't tell him about Ms. K's transformation, or fill him in on the robotic gnats, Flesh-skinner, or spiders. I certainly didn't tell him about the spiders talking. Right now, I needed this kid to come with me, not think that I was stark raving mad.

Even with the little I'd told him, Adri just stood there, breathing like a trapped animal.

Then he stiffened. "What if my parents are there... at the Zoo?" He spun around wildly. "We have to go find them!"

I gritted my teeth. Had this boy heard a word I said?

"Adri," I repeated slowly, "I have no idea where the Zoo is, other than 'somewhere in the mountains' and, if you're telling the truth, neither do you."

He looked at me with glazed eyes.

"But my parents..."

How could I break it to him? Whatever had happened, wherever they were, we couldn't help them. We could barely help ourselves.

I took a deep breath. "The best thing we can do for your parents is get back to the coast and get help."

Seconds passed like hours. I held his gaze until he steadied himself, looking at me with scared eyes.

He nodded once. "Okay."

We headed downstream along the riverbank, pushing through the narrow trees. They were ragged, with peeling white and grey bark, and branches that bowed low to the river. Long curtains of hair-like leaves stared sorrowfully at their own reflection, as if Adri and I needed to feel more depressed.

I glanced over my shoulder. He was way behind me, not keeping up, moving as slow as molasses.

"We have to hurry," I urged him.

He walked like someone in a dream. I resisted the urge to shake him. The dive into his memory had happened when I revived him on the mudflat. Whatever had caused it, maybe I shouldn't get too close.

"Adri!"

I was losing my patience. He was stumbling along behind me. We weren't getting anywhere. I thought of the broken key card that I'd shoved into one of my pockets. The Zoo's old research subjects were on the loose. Who knew what we would meet next? Yes, Adri had been through a lot, but if he really had no memory since the accident, then he didn't have a mental picture of what was waiting for us inside this forest.

I did.

We didn't have much time. Most predators hunted at night. We needed to get moving, but one look at Adri told me that my plan had backfired. Telling him that some wild animals had chased me wasn't making him move any faster. Instead, he looked ready to pass out. He paused after each step, scanning the trees, and jumping each time a bird flew overhead.

I slowed down slightly. If we were going to make it, I needed him to calm down. Maybe I could distract him, even a little, and get us out of here alive.

"So where are you from?" I tried.

Adri was looking over his shoulder so much, he nearly tripped over a snaky tree root.

"We'll make it somewhere safe if we don't brain ourselves first," I pointed out.

He blushed and tried to pick up the pace.

When I'd already forgotten the question, he stammered, "I grew up here in Trinidad... in Chaguanas. But I moved to New York when I was eight."

I'd been to Chaguanas with Da, past the abandoned cane fields at the heart of the island, to the roaring city centre packed with family-owned shops where you could get anything from a sari to an ATV, not to mention the banks, malls, convenience stores, massive market, street vendors and restaurants - from roti shops to fine dining and fast food - plus the busy maxi, taxi and bus stands crammed with people going to and coming from every part of the island.

It was the furthest thing from Samaan Bay, but then again, most places were.

Adri jumped as a lizard dashed across our path. I had to keep him talking and moving, or we'd never get anywhere. Right now, he looked like fourteen going on forty, but who could blame him? After hiking through the forest, life-threatening chases, falls, and no showers, we probably both looked like swamp-creatures.

"So, you come here a lot? Well, not here obviously," I waved at the green chaos around us, "but to Samaan Bay village?"

Adri didn't seem to hear me. He was busy flinching at the saw-music of a hidden band of cicadas.

"W-what? Um, no. First time back on the island in a while actually. My dad's family, the Khans, are from Naparima, but my mum's family is from near Samaan Bay. You know the Narines?"

I sighed and rolled my eyes. He'd been away too long.

"One point five million people in Trinidad – lots named Narine," I reminded him.

He flushed. "Right. Sorry. I just thought since you're from around here..."

"I'm not. I'm from Port of Spain."

"Oh, town girl!" he smiled slightly. You don't seem..."

"What?"

"Nothing," Adri faded, "you just seem to know what you're doing out here, that's all."

I thought of Da and everything he had taught me. Tears scratched the back of my throat. Okay, I needed to calm down, be less irritable. None of it was this kid's fault.

"Here are things you can't take back: the sped arrow, the spoken word..." Ms. Kofi loved to remind me.

I thought about her warning against talking to strangers and glanced at Adri sideways, while he concentrated on weaving through the trees. His arms were scrawny but strong. His nose was just like his mum's, tilted a little to the left in a way that was a charming and odd at the same time. Right now, though, the strain around his mouth and eyes showed watchfulness and fear.

We were lost and on the run from killer creatures. I couldn't see any way that he could be a threat, unless I counted his unbearable slowness. I bit back my irritation. It wouldn't hurt to find out more about him, and if that kept him moving one foot in front of the other, even better.

"So, you guys were here on holiday?" I asked lightly.

Adri hesitated, the tips of his ears going red.

That was not a hard question. Suspicion nibbled at the corners of my mind.

"Sorry for asking," I glanced at him with my eyebrows raised. "Here with the CIA, deep cover?"

He smiled for the first time. It made his drawn, tired face seem open and kind.

"Something like that," he threw back, grinning.

"Fine," I shrugged, as if it didn't matter.

His smile faded to an unhappy look. I let him catch up. It was better to keep him in front of me, just in case. I didn't have eyes in the back of my head.

Soon though, neither of us had the energy left to talk. I focused on breaking our way through leaves and brambles with my cutlass. Adri followed as closely as possible. He was slowing down again, so I decided to get ahead and set the pace. I'd worry about watching my back later.

The ground began sloping upward, pulling away from the river that grew slower and wider the further we walked. Uphill was hard going in our exhausted state. We were drained, drenched in sweat, not to mention hungry. I felt a cramp building in my legs. I could tell from Adri's pinched face that he couldn't make it much further either.

Finally, the ground was so steep that we were climbing, pulling ourselves up a bank of soil and rock by a web of tree roots. Sweat ran down my legs and arms like tiny streams. My palms were slick. Adri panted and struggled behind me. I grabbed an exposed tree root and pulled myself up onto a narrow ridge. He dragged himself up next to me.

"What...?" he coughed.

I was speechless.

We found ourselves looking down at a large sinkhole of a valley, wreathed in what looked like grey mist. The river limped through it to our left, down below.

There was just one small problem.

Everything in front of us had been destroyed.

Chapter Eight

FIND

Adri crouched over next to me, choking. The grey air wasn't mist or fog. It was bitter smoke that blew into our faces. I coughed, yanking the neck of my shirt up over my mouth and nose. Adri did the same. He and I looked at each other, then at the scene below.

If forests like this one were the lungs of the earth, then the earth was in trouble. It was as if the entire valley below us had been gouged out and dragged away. The rest of the forest was still standing, but within a space the size of a small village, nothing lived. There were no bushes, vines, shoots or trees, no grass or fallen leaves – only sand, dirt, and thick clouds of dusty smoke.

Tons of sand, gravel and stone had been dug out

and piled in towering cones across the valley floor. The river was so filled with mud and rocks that it ran in a series of brown pools. I could see gaping signs of the mudslides that afflicted this place when it rained. There were no trees to protect the land from washing away, or grass to help the rain seep into the earth. All that was left of the trees in the valley were charred stumps ripped out and lying on their sides, their gnarled roots grasping nothing but air.

Mora and palm, pine and cedar - the rings inside their trunks showed the decades they had taken to grow, all the changes they had seen and outlived, until now. Da had taught me that each tree had its own story. But someone had plowed them down without a care. Even a grove of poui trees had been felled, their yellow flowers trampled in the dirt like wasted gold. Anger and sadness burned the back of my throat.

On the far side of the hole, I could see piles of logs. From those mounds, long trails stretched across the sand, up the loose sides of the valley and into the surrounding forest. Whoever had cut down and beheaded the trees had started the process of dragging them away, probably to a lumberyard or factory.

Without a word, Adri and I began inching our way to the right, around the edge of the valley, in the direction of the trails, careful not to slip down the steep sides of the crater. These might not be the people we were looking for, but loggers and quarry workers could still help get us to safety. The valley and surrounding forest were quiet, with no sound of people at work, but if we followed the trails left by the logs, we were sure to find someone. Despite our looted surroundings, my heart began to sing at the thought of getting home.

A short way ahead of us, down on the valley floor, was a mound that was smaller than the piles of logs. As we moved in that direction, the wind turned, and blew a horrific smell into our faces.

"What is that?" Adri heaved.

I couldn't answer him. I was busy retching, trying to block my nose and mouth. The hairs on the back of my neck stood up. The smell was the stench of rotting creatures and burnt flesh. The smallest hill on the valley floor was a pile of smouldering animals.

My insides hurt.

"Who did this?" Adri whispered in horror.

I had no idea. I'd read about companies doing large-scale logging, quarrying, or drilling for oil in the Amazon rainforest in South America, using force to move protesters, Indigenous tribes, and villages out of their way. They destroyed the rich plant and animal life of the forest – living creatures that might hold the cure for Alzheimer's or cancer, not to mention that they maintained the delicate balance of life on earth. But I didn't know that anything like this was happening here.

"Maybe we should go a different way," I suggested to Adri.

I squinted my eyes and fought not to breathe deeply as the wind picked up, flinging the smell of charred rot back into my face.

Now I wasn't sure if the people who had done this would see us as kids to be rescued, or as witnesses who needed to be shut up.

"Zo, look," Adri warned.

I saw it too: movement on the far side of the valley. It was a brown stream curling out of the forest, down into the crater, moving toward the river. There was no rain, no sound of running water, but it moved quickly and smoothly, unlike the bloated channel in the middle of the valley. And unlike any stream I had ever seen, it had appeared out of nowhere. I could swear it hadn't been there before.

"Huh! Huh!"

What was that sound?

In a split second, I realised that it was Adri. I dragged him down to the ground at the edge of the valley. He was hyperventilating loudly. If I didn't shut him up right away, he was going to attract that thing's attention and get us both killed. I slapped my hand over his nose and mouth. His eyes asked questions I couldn't answer. I just knew that we needed to be more silent than we'd ever been. Lying on my stomach, I stared back out over the valley.

Just as suddenly as it had come out of the trees, the stream stopped. One end of it lifted into the air, turning from side to side. I pressed my face into the ground next to Adri. Pebbles dug into my face. That wasn't a stream. It was the only thing alive in the valley – something massive and long and sinewy, like an enormous snake. I looked again and it began to seep into the forest on the far side of the valley, in a different direction from the way it had come, but thankfully, not toward us.

The last inch of whatever-it-was disappeared into the trees, but I kept my hand clamped over Adri's mouth. I could feel him take panicked breaths through his nose. He looked at me and I let him know with my eyes that if he made a single sound, it was over for us both. I counted a full five minutes, giving the thing time to move away into the forest on the other side of the crater. Or so I hoped. Then, I grabbed Adri and climbed back down the embankment, away from the valley, as quickly and quietly as we could.

We got down to the forest floor in record time. Then we were running without any clear direction other than away from the danger behind us. My heart slammed into the walls of my chest. Neither of us could talk. The thing we'd just seen was longer than the Flesh-skinner, with a snake-like shape and movement. If something like that caught us in the forest, it was over. So, we ran.

After what felt like forever, we had put some space between us and the valley, but I still couldn't bring myself to stop running. Adri seemed to have the same idea, because he was ducking under branches and jumping over roots like he was on an obstacle course at the Olympics. Even with my shorter legs, I wasn't about to be left behind. I dashed between the trees next to him, fighting to pick up speed, ignoring the stitch in my side. The ground was rising again, gradually at first, then more sharply.

Soon, we were forced to slow to a walk. We were exhausted and the slope was painfully steep. My legs were on fire. With every step, I bit back sobs. I could hear Adri fighting for breath next to me. Finally, we came to the top of the rise – a green hilltop, covered with large spreading trees. The air was cool. Breeze rustled through the leaves, but we felt far from peaceful.

"What was that? What was that?" Adri paced back and forth, raking his hands over his spiky hair. "That thing was huge!"

"I don't know," I answered as calmly as I could, "but there's more..."

I told him about Ms. Kofi's transformation into a giant spider, about the metallic gnats, the Flesh-skinner in all its gory detail, the talking spiders, including the one with the mechanical arm, and finally, my suspicion that they'd all come from the Zoo. When I was finished, his eyes and mouth were giant 'O's'. I could see doubt, fear, and shock play tug of war on his face.

The only thing I held back was the part about falling into one of his memories. I couldn't imagine what he would think I was, if I told him about that part now. I needed him to trust me for us to get out of this forest alive, and saying that I might have an uncontrolled, mind-entering ability probably wasn't the best way to build that trust. Besides, from the expression on Adri's face, it seemed like what I'd told him was already more than enough for his mind to process in one day.

"So, you see, even if your parents are at the Zoo," I said finally, "we'd have to find it. Then how would we get them out on our own, with those things on the loose?"

He sat down heavily. I stood there, waiting. At first, he stared at me as if I were lying or crazy. Then slowly, his expression changed to one of stunned acceptance.

"If I hadn't seen what I just saw in that valley, I would think you were nuts," he admitted quietly, "but I saw what I saw."

"Me too," I said, shaking my head, "even though I wish I could un-see it."

He stared up at me. "What do we do now?"

"How should I know?" I snapped.

Why was I the leader of this little expedition?

"Okay, fine," Adri frowned, "but it's getting late." He pointed to the sky. The sun was low, stretching shadows along the ground. "We have to find somewhere safe for the night."

For some reason, my stepdad Jake came to mind. One of his watchwords was "Help first, debate later." That man was annoying, but to be fair, he was always the first to do what was needed for Mum, Baby Tayo, and me... And I'd never even thanked him. I tried to shake the guilt. I would tell him when I got back alive. For now, I had to figure this situation out, for Adri's sake and mine.

I looked around. "Let's get something to eat and climb into the highest tree we can find."

Adri nodded, relieved. Around us, manakin birds in blue, red, yellow, and green, chirped and whistled through the air. When I saw what was attracting the birds' attention, for the first time in days, I felt something like joy. They were gathering on a pois doux tree.

Adri moved slowly, like a damaged robot, shaking the dirt and stones out of his shoes.

"Padoo," I announced triumphantly, pointing to the tree, "pois doux."

I picked up some of the fruit and gave it to him. He took it gingerly, checking out its bean-pod shape.

"Like this," I cracked the large pod in two, revealing what looked like small wads of cotton in a row inside. I popped one of those white segments into my mouth and sucked off the juicy pulp, then spit the smooth black seed out on the ground. Adri slipped a piece of the fruit into his mouth. I laughed as his eyes opened wide.

"What!" he spluttered.

It tasted like vanilla ice cream.

Soon, our mouths were too full to talk. There was a balata tree nearby as well, its spiky trunk oozing gummy sap. Ripe balata covered the ground under the tree in a bright orange carpet. We picked up as many as we could, devouring the sweet insides of each round fruit and spitting out the seeds. The balata were so small that we had to eat a bunch of them to take the edge off our hunger, but between that and the pois doux, we had dinner.

While Adri kept eating, I looked around. Our shadows were long, the light golden. Sunset was coming and with it, danger. We had to find shelter fast. The balata tree was too tall and spiky to climb and the pois doux's branches were too close to the ground. Just beyond both trees, a large umbrella of leaves caught my eye. It was a samaan tree – twin to the one on Rain-Tree Hill, with a strong Y-shaped trunk. That was it. We could spend the night here.

Adri tossed the empty fruit skins away. I watched the light bronze the tips of the trees. Our next-door neighbours, a flock of green and yellow parrots, squawked goodnight. They rustled noisily and flapped away, releasing a shower of cracked seeds.

Adri looked up at the spreading branches of the Rain-Tree with doubtful eyes.

"Is that safe?"

"Let's find out," I challenged him.

We didn't have much choice.

My 'HERE' t-shirt had seen better days, but thankfully, around my waist, I still had what was left of my long-sleeved cotton shirt.

"We can each tie ourselves to a branch with this shirt and take turns sleeping, okay? You first," I ordered.

Adri's spindly legs climbed the tree slowly, with lots of stops and starts. He sat on a low branch and reached down to help me.

"I got it, thanks," I grunted, pleased to see his surprise as I pulled myself up smoothly on my own.

We climbed to the highest point we could, until the branches above us were too thin to trust. I settled myself into a crook of the tree, facing the trunk, with a branch beneath me. Adri took a similar spot on a branch nearby.

"You okay?" I asked him.

"Yeah," he decided, looking gangly and awkward on his perch, "snug as a bug in a rug."

I couldn't help but laugh. He did too.

"I mean, everyone should camp like this, right?" he teased.

"Yup," I whipped back, "tents and sleeping bags are overrated."

He grinned.

Seeing Adri in the last light, I wondered again why his family had shaved off all their hair. I tried to imagine how people would've reacted to me in Samaan Bay if I'd arrived there bald. The new growth on Adri's head added an unexpected toughness to his face. His eyes, however, were long and a little uneven, giving him a curious, even mischievous look.

He was two years older than me, but he was slimmer and more wiry than I was. Swimming and gymnastics had added muscles to my already solid frame. I was what Trinis called "thick". At times, I'd wanted to be long and thin. like most of the women I saw in movies and magazines, but the last few days in the forest had made me realize just how strong I really was. I gave my body silent thanks for getting me this far.

"We should take turns sleeping," I reminded Adri, trying to hand him the shirt to tie himself to the branch beneath him. "You first."

"It's fine," he countered, "I can stay up for a while."

I angled my head to look at him. "Didn't you drown today?"

His teeth flashed in a grim smile. "Good point."

Chapter Nine

WATCH

My eyes flew open. It was pitch black. How long had I been asleep? I blinked slowly, adjusting to the darkness. Thankfully, I was still sitting on a branch, leaning on the wide tree trunk in front of me. I looked down. It was a long way to fall.

Adri! I peered in his direction. I could just see his shape. He was still on a branch, leaning against the tree trunk, motionless, asleep. I felt a mixture of relief and anger at myself for not keeping watch. Not like there was much to see. The moon was hidden behind clouds. I heard the whirring, eerie clicks and high-pitched cries of creatures passing through the night.

"You up?" Adri whispered, without turning his head.

"Yes, you?" I stammered, glad that he couldn't see my face.

"Can't sleep..." his voice trickled away.

An image of the Flesh-skinner invaded my mind: its rotten-fish smell and hot slimy breath.

"So, was it a bet, shaving your head?" I asked Adri, trying to shake my thoughts.

The silence was so long that I began to wonder if he'd heard me.

"Nah," he said lightly, "just my mom's chemo."

I didn't know what to say.

He cleared his throat. "Ma's hair grew back though. She donated it just before we flew down. Dad and I jumped in too."

"Oh," I said, seeing the glow on the faces of his parents in the memory I'd crashed into against my will.

It all made sense now.

"Ma's one year cancer free," Adri announced proudly, his voice shaking slightly.

"Wow," I said, kicking myself for prying. Why had I been so suspicious of him all this time?

"Yeah," he went on, "this was our trip to celebrate... As you can see, that's going well."

Crazy laughter burst from my mouth.

I slapped my hand over my lips.

"Sorry!" What was wrong with me?

"Don't be," he assured me. "Pity sucks."

That was when we really started talking.

He told me about his dad playing his mom's favorite 90s hip-hop in the hospital room after her surgery, while a young oncologist with stunning dreadlocks hummed along to Erykah Badu, Missy Elliott and Lauryn Hill.

I told him how my baby brother Tayo could bring us all scrambling to his room with one dramatic shriek, then give a satisfied super-villain smile from his crib like, "Gotcha!"

Adri shared that on days when his mom found it hard to get out of bed, she would ask him to read from her well-worn, gilt-edged collection of poems by Rumi. His dad would make zaffrani soup in the kitchen two doors down, filling the air with the bright smell of ginger, spicy garlic and the warm aroma of saffron. They'd hear him singing along - loud and off-key - to soft rock, chutney soca, Mumbai love songs, or old-time calypso, depending on his mood and how Ma's chemo had gone that day. And she would mouth Rumi's words along with Adri from memory: *These pains you feel are messengers, listen to them.*

He said that Queens, where they lived, had everything and everyone from around the world, but he didn't feel the same way in his new school on the Upper East Side. Sometimes it felt strange to be the scholarship kid with the accent hardly anyone at school recognised, who was from an island that was nothing but a dot on their maps.

"Things you only miss when you leave here, you know?"

He cracked me up with his take on all the Trini uses of the phrase "Eh-eh!" including appreciation of a juicy piece of gossip, shock, sarcasm, joy, horror, affection, disgust, intense approval, or an absolute no, depending on how it was said.

"The truth is," he admitted quietly, "there were some good kids in my class, but I didn't tell anyone Ma was sick. I told myself I didn't want to deal with their questions, but really, I just didn't feel like having one more thing that made me different, you know?"

I nodded in the dark. "At least you didn't take it out on anyone else. I've been mean to my mum's husband, Jake. He's never been anything but kind to me and respectful of Mum, Da and I, but sometimes just seeing him makes me think of everything that's gone, you know? Sometimes, I just want the old things back."

"I feel you," Adri said, "change is... weird. Even when Ma started to get better, it was hard to believe it was real, until it was."

I liked that he didn't try to console me, or give me advice, the way most people did when you told them about something rough you'd been through. He just listened, and I did the same.

We talked and talked, until finally, there was a moment of silence between us.

Then, for the first time that night, I felt awkward. Maybe I'd said too much. I wondered if he was thinking the same thing.

The moon was behind clouds again and I could barely see him in the dark. I could hear a high wind picking up in the distance. Adri was totally, painfully, silent.

"Look," I told him, "I hope this doesn't make..."

"Shhh," he hissed.

Then I heard it. That wasn't the wind. A high scream pierced the forest. I nearly lost my grip on the branch. The Flesh-skinner was out hunting. A long wail chased the silence. It was getting closer. I hoped Adri wouldn't make another sound.

The moon came out of hiding at the worst time. Just then, the Flesh-skinner crawled out of the gloom, its wet skin glistening. It paced up the hill and slunk through the trees toward us. It seemed to smell us right away and headed straight for our tree, snarling and scuffling at its base, looking up at us with red, hungry eyes.

I stared down and the Flesh-skinner held me in its gaze, with the sly eyes of something that had lived long and seen a great many things. Before I could blink, it spun around and slammed its long, spiked tail into the trunk of the tree.

"Adri, hold on!" I shouted, grabbing the branch beneath me with my legs and arms.

The Rain-Tree shuddered. I clung to my shivering branch and could see Adri out of the corner of my eye, desperately doing the same thing. The Flesh-skinner screamed. Green slime flew from its jaws. It went up onto its hind legs and clawed at the trunk of the tree, getting as much height as it could, sending chunks of bark flying through the air. Its massive jaws ripped off the lower branches and snapped them like twigs. The tree shook hard, releasing a shower of pods and leaves. I felt light-headed and tightened my grip on the branch. I prayed that Adri was doing the same. The Flesh-skinner howled with rage, hitting the tree again and again. All I could do was close my eyes and hold on.

"Zo! You okay?" Adri shouted.

"I'm alright," I answered weakly.

The shaking had stopped. I opened my eyes slowly. We were both alive. The tree was battered, its trunk scarred, but it was still standing. Best of all, the Flesh-skinner couldn't climb.

I bit the inside of my lip in relief. The Flesh-skinner turned its back to the tree, eyes glinting like rubies. Was it going to give up and leave? I'd read an article online about two girls in the Andaman Islands. They were trapped in a tree overhanging a river, stalked by a huge crocodile. It had stayed beneath their tree all night, waiting for them to lose hold. Perhaps the Flesh-skinner had the same idea. It would wait for one or both of us to lose our grip, then... I thought of my parents, wondering forever what had happened to me, not even finding my bones.

I trembled in a sudden fit of cold. Lightning flashed across the sky. Rain gushed down. I could see the Flesh-skinner's ghostly outline and shining red eyes. Its breath was like the rumble of a train.

"Hold on!" I screamed to Adri, just in time.

The Flesh-skinner attacked the Rain-Tree with a new intensity, headbutting the trunk. I clung to my see-saw branch, head reeling. The wind whipped around my ears and the rain poured as the tree creaked and moaned under the beast's blows. The leaves of the Rain-Tree had already folded in two, offering us no protection from the storm. Within seconds, I was drenched to the bone, trembling with fear and cold. I could tell that Adri was too.

The Flesh-skinner was relentless. It slammed its tail into the 'V' of the tree, where the trunk spread in two directions.

"Look out!" Adri yelled.

One of the higher boughs came crashing down, colliding with my branch and nearly sending me tumbling into the Flesh-skinner's jaws. I screamed, holding on to the branch for dear life. The beast leapt at my dangling feet.

"Zo!" I could see Adri trying to climb across to help me.

"No! Go back!" I screamed, fighting to pull myself back up.

Before he could reach me, I was back up on the branch. I wrapped my arms and legs around it as tightly as I could. Adri froze where he was, holding on. My body was slick with rain. The wind roared, drowning out the Flesh-skinner's frustrated cries.

Soon, the darkness paled just enough for me to see Adri's terrified eyes and the Flesh-skinner's snarling face. My heart dropped as it slammed its long, ridged tail into the place where the Rain-Tree's trunk branched in two. Bits of wood and bark flew up. I held on through each shock, my arms and legs too stiff with cramps to move. I could hear Adri groan. Again and again, with frantic blows, the beast hit the same spot with the force of an axe.

Creeeeeak. I couldn't believe my eyes. After all it had withstood, the base of the tree was splintering. If this kept up, the trunk would split, sending Adri, me, and the tree crashing down to the Flesh-skinner below. I held on tight, but it didn't matter. In a few minutes, it would be over. There was nothing more that we could do.

The Flesh-skinner yelped, probably stuck by a shard of wood. Then it began growling, lashing the tree with even more force. I looked over at Adri. His eyes were glued to the Flesh-skinner. I was numb. A hazy light began creeping up the hill. I could see the sun now, creeping over the distant horizon. The tree shuddered as the beast screamed up at us. I smelled its rank breath. Blood beat in my ears, but other than that, I felt nothing. My whole life so far, my parents' divorce, Jake and the new baby, the move to Samaan Bay; it had all come down to this.

There was a loud cracking noise. My side of the tree began to tilt. The Flesh-skinner whined in anticipation, or so I thought. I looked down and my body clenched with shock. In the growing light, I could see the Flesh-skinner's back steaming and bubbling like water in a pot. It spun in circles, swinging its tail left and right. It wasn't whining with excitement. It was crying out in pain.

The Flesh-skinner's skin erupted into angry bruises as the sun inched up over the horizon. A flash went through me. Sunlight! The Flesh-skinner couldn't stand the sun! As warmth and light filled the air, its skin burned and peeled. It began crawling backwards to the far side of the clearing, staring at us bitterly. Soon its eyes were almost swollen shut. The Flesh-skinner's entire body was covered with sores. It twisted and writhed in pain. The lesions grew worse as the sun climbed higher. Loud snarls rose to a high-pitched cry. Finally, with one swift jerk, the Flesh-skinner sped away and disappeared down the side of the hill, back into the forest. From my perch, I could see a line of trees nodding and waving in its wake. I followed the dancing trees well into the distance, until they went too far for me to see.

"Is it really gone?" Adri wondered.

It seemed that way, for now.

I stared at the forest in the direction that the Flesh-skinner had taken, straining for any sign of movement in the trees. The rising sun flushed the sky orange, pink and gold. The world woke up to the loud piping of birds.

Somewhere the Flesh-skinner was resting, out of the sunlight, waiting for another night to fall.

Chapter Ten

FIGHT

"Adri," I whispered, shaking.

In the half-light, he looked younger than he was – like a boy surprised to find that he wasn't dreaming. I wondered if I looked just as lost.

"Time to get down," I said, giving my voice a strength I didn't feel.

Adri groaned, still clutching the branch under him.

From up here, in what was left of the tree, I tried to figure out where we were in the forest. I could just catch glimpses of a river away to our right, with rocky hills in the distance beyond it. It seemed that in our mad dash from Dead Valley we had run away from the river, instead of towards it. Now we needed to head east to get back. It was dawn, so the sun was in the east. In the absence of a compass, we'd have to follow it as best as we could.

My arms and legs ached. I could barely feel my fingers and toes after lying curled around the tree branch for so long. I clenched and unclenched my fists, flexing my feet to get the blood moving through my cramped muscles. That was when I heard the tree creak and felt the branch beneath me tilt under my weight. I moved forward carefully toward the trunk of the tree, but it gave an ominous moan.

"Adri, move!" I shouted, sliding down as fast as I could.

Half of the tree was coming down with me. The Flesh-skinner had practically cracked it in two. I didn't even have time to look for Adri, but I could hear him scrambling down behind me. The last few feet were a blur of leaves and crashing branches. I closed my eyes and jumped for the ground below. When I opened them, I was lying on the damp earth, face down under a pile of twigs and leaves. My body was sore, but I could see, and most importantly, move.

"Zo..." Adri muttered nearby.

"You okay?" we asked each other at the same time.

I sat up slowly. He was lying tangled in some boughs on my left, with a silly grin on his face. Whether from exhaustion or relief, we both started laughing hysterically.

We pushed the foliage away and crawled out into the sunlight.

The massive Rain-Tree was a wreck. Most of its leaves were gone and its left side lay on the ground around us. Yet I could see that part of the trunk was still rooted in earth. The remaining branches stretched up to the sky. I thought of its sister-tree on Rain-Tree Hill, in all its lonely beauty. Hopefully, there was enough of this one left to grow.

Adri stood next to me, staring at the destruction, his face solemn.

"Thank you," I murmured to the tree.

I told Adri about seeing the river east of us. We ate as much balata and pois doux as we could, then set off in the direction of the sun.

At first, we were both too sore to talk. We walked like unoiled tin men. At least the way we were going seemed safe; none of the trees bore the broken branches and green slime of the Flesh-skinner. All we could hope was that it was far away, hiding from the light. However, as I thought about Samaan Bay, a horrible thought slithered into my mind. What if, on one of the nights since I'd been gone, the Flesh-skinner had slunk down to the village?

According to Jake, a few years ago, the fishing in Samaan Bay had dropped to almost nothing because of overfishing and pollution in other parts of the sea. When the fish wouldn't come back, most of the young people left Samaan Bay to look for jobs. For Jake's company to build the island's first green smelter there, they'd had to source workers from other areas. Those who stayed overnight slept in wooden barracks at one end of the village. Apart from them, there were mainly children and old people in Samaan Bay. None of them, except maybe Ms. K in spider form, were a match for the Flesh-skinner.

My stomach rolled. What if the beast had gone to the cottage at the edge of the forest, after Ms. K had gone home for the night? If Mum, Jake and the baby were outside as darkness closed in, they wouldn't have known what hit them.

Suddenly, I was choking and running.

I could hear Adri chasing after me calling, "What is it? Zo!"

"Don't touch me!" I bent over shaking. "I need to warn my family about that thing before..." I couldn't finish the thought.

My baby brother's heart-shaped face filled my mind: his dark sapodilla-seed eyes and lopsided dimples, his loud, gurgling laugh. I'd called him the Terror for most of his life, resented the attention he got from our mum. Now I just needed to see him alive.

After a while, I realised that Adri was standing near me with a look of concern cut into his face. "It's okay Zo. It'll be okay."

How would he know? He didn't even know where his parents were.

Somehow though, his voice soothed me. I breathed slowly, straightened up, and looked at his weary face. To even have a chance of getting back to my family, I had to believe that he was right.

"Okay," I said, trying to convince myself, "let's go."

After what felt like hours, we had a win. We both rushed toward it at the same time: the glorious sound of running water. The river was just ahead, restored to its former size, guarded by white-barked trees. My heart rose like a kite. We dashed to the edge of the water and drank our fill, only just realizing how thirsty we'd been. We washed our faces, heads, and arms in the cool water. Then we kept walking on the bank, downstream. We were back on track, grinning like little kids. We might get out of here in one piece after all.

Adri seemed much better than the day before. We were both sports fanatics so, as we walked, we argued about the World Cup and the best teams to ever lift the trophy. We ranked the new stars coming from around the world. We boasted about the West Indian big hitters in Premier League cricket and raved about the game-changing tennis of the Williams sisters.

"What do you want to study?" I asked him.

For me, it was Ecology and Languages, so I could travel around the world like my dad, but to set up clean, renewable energy.

When Adri said "Archaeology" that jump-started a whole conversation about Ancient Egyptian hieroglyphs.

We even forgot to be quiet, chatting loudly as we moved through the trees. It was like having one of my talks with Da.

"Yeah," Adri reminded me, "what we call mummification was the Pharaohs trying to keep themselves together, even after death."

"Ms. K says you can't take it with you, but then again she turned out to be a Giant Spider so..." I gave one dry laugh and ducked under a broken branch sprouting new leaves. "I have a great-aunt who always quotes: 'Once to die and after that the judgment.'"

I glanced over at Adri, the words dying on my lips. "Oh."

We needed to change the topic, fast. The excitement had leaked from his face. I could tell that all this talk about life and death was making him think about his parents.

I signalled to him quickly. He stopped, half-crouched, eyes wide. I pointed up at the nearest tree. It took him a while to spot it among the shifting leaves: a miniature dinosaur lying on a branch above us, with iridescent scales in shades of green, yellow and brown. Its long tail hung completely still. The pouch under its neck and the pointed spikes on its back looked like a royal headdress. Its round eyes watched us closely.

"Iguana," I whispered.

A king of its kind. Or maybe among lizards there were no kings.

A sudden rustling disturbed the stillness. I could feel Adri freeze next to me. There was no time to hide. After an unbearable second, six animals rushed out of the trees a short distance ahead. They looked like giant guinea pigs, furry and brown, with curious rabbit faces, mouse ears and round rumps with no tails.

"Agouti," I exhaled.

"Do they bite?" Adri stared at their plump bodies as they scrambled into the safety of the undergrowth.

"It's okay," I laughed, "plants and fruit only."

They were probably going to the river for a drink. I'd caught a glimpse of an agouti on hikes with my dad before. We were lucky to see so many now. Da said they were at risk from too much clearing the forest and hunting. I thought of the dead valley we'd seen.

Adri chuckled quietly as the smallest agouti poked its fat-cheeked face out of the bushes to stare at us for one last time, before scampering back to the others.

"They're cute," he smiled.

I was just glad they were still around.

"Want to know how the agouti lost its tail?" I asked Adri as I walked ahead, thinking about the story Mum had told me as a child.

"Watch out!" he grabbed at my arm.

"No!" I flinched away, avoiding his grip, terrified of falling into another one of his memories.

In the process, I nearly stepped on a macajuel snake curled up into a figure eight, with brown markings that looked like dried leaves on the forest floor. Thankfully, it was only a baby that quickly slid away.

"A snake," Adri stated the obvious, giving me a hurt look.

I avoided his confused gaze and kept going forward more carefully, on the lookout for snakes and scorpions. My reaction must have seemed strange, but I couldn't explain it to him. How would that sound? 'I'm afraid that if you grab my arm, I'll fall into another one of your memories.'

Right. No.

What would happen if I told Adri about being trapped in his memory the last time he'd held my arm, on the mudflat by the river where he'd nearly drowned? I could already see the fear that would take over his face, as he wondered who, and what, I really was.

Now, in response to his unspoken question about why I'd batted his hand away, I set my face like stone and picked up the pace. We'd been too relaxed, talked too much. It was time to focus. Adri and I didn't need to be best friends right now. We needed to get out of this forest. The sooner we did that, the better.

Suddenly, there was a loud crack in the leaves above us.

Before either of us could react, something like thick lengths of white string slid down from the trees. I looked up in slow motion, unable to guess what was coming next. There, crawling down the long lines of web toward us, were the spiders from the ravine.

"Ay girlie!" Cap'n Peg called. "You still out here?"

A spider with a backward baseball cap made some comment about humans getting lost so easily, they couldn't find their own tails in the dark.

The others giggled, while a tiny spider who was trying to look cool in cracked aviator sunglasses whispered curiously, "They have tails?"

Adri stared at me, petrified. It was one thing to hear about talking spiders, another thing to have them crawl toward you in the forest.

'Run,' I mouthed silently at him, pulling out my cutlass and getting ready to sprint.

"Whoa!" Cap'n Peg warned.

Thwack! The cutlass was webbed out of my hands into the canopy overhead.

Half of the spiders jumped to form a circle around us. The rest guarded us from their webs. There was nowhere to go.

"Relax girlie," Cap'n Peg rolled her one red eye, "we not here for you and your new," she gave Adri a cutting look, "friend."

"Yeah!" the other spiders chimed in. "We not here for you."

"Crazy Two-legs," a spider in a tie-dyed tutu blew a huge ball of matching gum close to my face, "think every time they pass wind, is a hurricane."

The spiders howled with laughter.

"Leave us alone!" Adri yelled.

I signalled to him to be still. Now that we couldn't escape, there was no point in riling them up against us.

Cap'n Peg threw a withering look all around. "Like I was saying, we have our own business to attend to."

I backed towards Adri as a bunch of spiders came forward, holding something squirming and fighting between them. They parted to reveal... the coat that Old Man Yancy had been wearing in the market, made of a thousand different scraps of fabric.

Adri and I were shocked silent. Now, I knew that what I'd seen back in Samaan Bay was real. The heat hadn't played tricks on my eyes. Right in front of me, the coat was leashed by webs held by spiders on either side. Yet it moved on its own, fighting and twisting against the spiders' webs. In fact, not only did the coat not stay still, but it kept silently and ferociously changing shape, struggling to break free. One second, it was a dog with sharp bared teeth, the next a tiger trying to pounce, a bucking donkey, a striking snake.

Each time it changed, the spiderwebs immediately adjusted to keep it in place. It couldn't get out.

"Th-the old man," I stuttered when I could finally speak. "Mr. Yancy, where is he?"

"Fugitive on the run," Cap'n Peg smiled grimly, "but not for long, now that we have his pet."

I was relieved that he hadn't been caught. But were the spiders after him because he'd tried to warn me about Ms. K? Somehow, it didn't seem like a smart question to ask out loud.

"What are you going to do with it?" I demanded instead, pointing to the coat that was heaving silently like it was out of breath.

"We're taking it back to HQ, for the Council!" the little runt with cracked aviators piped up.

There was a stunned silence from the others.

The tiny spider cowered as Cap'n Peg swung around to face it, snarling; "You never heard the saying, 'Loose lips sink ships?'"

"Headquarters, the Council? What's that?" Adri jumped in.

The other spiders cowered as Cap'n Peg slid down her web, right in front of Adri's face. Her mechanical arm twitched and whirred next to his nose. I tensed up silently, ready to jump in. Adri stepped back as far as he could without touching the spiders standing guard behind him.

"That, my boy, is for me to know, and for the likes of you to find out," Cap'n Peg snarled. She turned and spat a wad of green slime on the ground nearby.

"Let's just stay calm," I suggested, in what I hoped was a calm voice. Adri looked like he was panicking. I needed him to stop asking questions that could get us both killed.

"Adri," I reminded him through gritted teeth, "remember I told you about Ms. K? She's their boss, she's in charge."

Cap'n Peg gave me a solemn look. "Even the Boss

has bosses girlie. It's the way of the world."

I shuddered at the thought of anyone who
dare try to boss Ms. K around.

Cap'n Peg shook her head as if reading my tho[u]
Her smile was far from comforting: "So girlie, yo[u]
safe, y'hear? The only thing you need to know a[bout]
The Council is that the Zoo is their place."

Great. The Council was in charge of the Zoo[ ]
still running it in secret? My stomach churned. [I]
should definitely stop asking questions.

Cap'n Peg snapped at the other spiders, "Time[ ]
move out!"

They sprang back into action, muttering to eac[h]
other. "You ent see Little Eniya nearly cause b[ig]
trouble? Me, I almost pee my pants. I not cut o[ut]
for that kind of static!"

The tiny spider I assumed was Little Eniya st[ood]
sobbing softly in a corner, being comforted [by a]
motherly spider with a big brooch and flow[ery]
scarf. The others were busy following Cap'n[ ]
barked orders. Several spiders had to hol[d]
replace the webs around the renegade coat. [It was]
changing shape again and fighting to fre[e]
becoming by turns, a lunging bear, a sn[apping]
caiman, and scratching hawk.

Adri and I pulled back slowly, not sure wh
to run and risk attracting the spiders' attention.
Then we were too busy staring to run.

Eight spiders, under Cap'n Peg's direction,
jumped between two trees that were several feet
apart and started weaving a large, patterned web
between the trunks. It was finished in seconds and
when it was, Cap'n Peg swung over. She touched
the central point of the web with the tip of one
of her non-mechanical legs. As she did, the web
began to shimmer silver, then translucent. Out of
nowhere came the quiet, steady sound of drums.

"What's happening?" Adri whispered.

I had no idea.

The web that was stretched between the two
trees now looked like a mirror, but instead of
reflecting us and the surrounding forest, it was
filled with something like fog. Inside of the web,
through the fog, I could catch glimpses of a long
wall on a hill. It was in the distance, but growing
closer, like a video camera zooming in. Before I
could think, the spiders ran in groups of threes
and fives and jumped right into the web. They
scampered up the hill and over the wall, out of
sight.

An electric current ran through my body. It dawned on me what I was seeing.

The web in front of us was a portal to somewhere else.

While I stood there reeling, the spiders kept jumping into the web, disappearing over the wall in the fog. As the wall grew closer, I could see that it was made of towering cement, topped with barbed wire, built for keeping things out, or in.

I turned to Adri. Like me, his jaw hung open.

The spiders in front of us dragged the squirming coat toward the web. My heart sank but I didn't know what to do. The coat writhed and fought and changed shape, but it couldn't get free. Despite its relentless struggle, the spiders yanked it into the portal, over the massive wall and out of sight, to whatever lay beyond.

The wall kept getting closer. I could see now that the barbed wire was rusty, and twisted in parts, covered with vines and lichen. I could just make out a sign on the wall that grew clearer every second. Soon, I could see two words.

Adri read them aloud: "GLOBAL...CENTR..."

"Zo! It's the Zoo!" he yelled.

"Adri..." I tried warning him.

My mouth was dry. A sense of dread crawled up my neck. The last of the spiders leapt through the portal, except for Cap'n Peg. She turned and waved her mechanical arm.

"Bon voyage!" she cheered, then froze.

"My parents," Adri roared, sprinting toward her, "are they in there?"

Cap'n Peg's face hardened. She raised her mechanical arm and aimed it at Adri's chest. "Come on then. Try and find out!"

He was going to jump into the web portal.

"Wait!" Without thinking, I ran after him and launched myself through the air.

I slammed into him, knocking him off course. We rolled along the ground. He shoved me away and scrambled to his feet. I sat up slowly.

Around us was nothing but forest. The river bubbled behind strangely silent trees.

We were in the same spot where the spiders had met us, but Cap'n Peg, her crew, the web, and the Zoo, were all gone.

Chapter Eleven

LEAVE

Adri stood there with his back to me, in the place where the portal had been. His fists were clenched. The silence was unbearable.

"Adri, I'm sor..."

He spun towards me; face twisted with rage.

"We don't even know what's in there!" I stammered, as he stormed across the space between us.

He towered over me; his face hard like the rocks of the ravine I'd been trapped in when I first met the spiders. His eyes cut into my pleading face.

"Look Adri, I was trying to..."

"THAT WASN'T YOUR DECISION TO MAKE!" he roared. Then softly, heartbrokenly, he whispered, "What if they were in there – my parents?"

"We'll get help and come back for them. I promise!"

Shame and guilt raked over me like hot coals. What if I was wrong?

I braced myself when Adri opened his mouth.

Then he slammed his jaw shut and stormed away into the forest, in the direction we had been going.

I stood there, rooted to the spot, thinking about the crazy dive into his memory that had happened when I first met him. Maybe I could do it again, but this time, by choice. I could go back into his memories and find out what had happened to him and his parents.

I shook my head. Whatever had happened to his family must've been major, or they would never have left their only son. Even if I could go back into Adri's memories and he believed what I saw, there was nothing we could do. If his parents were at the Zoo, or somewhere else in the forest, the only way for us to help them was to help ourselves. Once we got to a village, I could try re-entering Adri's memories to get the information we needed to find them.

I ran to catch up with him. He didn't slow down or speed up. He just acted like I wasn't there. Neither of us spoke. It grew hotter and hotter, until we walked in a daze. Invisible insects buzzed around our heads. I was starving and I was sure he was too. The only edible thing I could find was cocorite, littering the ground under a random tree. We picked the yellow bullet-shaped fruit up off the ground and peeled the shells off with our teeth, but the fruit was almost all seed. After a few tries, I threw them down with disgust, hungrier than when I'd started eating.

The air around us was damp and suffocating. I felt like I was covered with the musky, leafy smell of the forest.

Adri stood there, gnawing at cocorite.

"Come on," I urged him, "we have to hurry. Let's try and make it out before nightfall."

"What makes you think we will?" he muttered under his breath, bending down to collect a few more seeds.

"What?" I snapped.

"Other than 'by the river', do you have any idea where we are right now?" He straightened up and looked at me. His eyes were dark, jaw clenched.

"Okay genius, so what's your plan?" I threw back, shaking with anger and my own doubt.

Adri ignored me and kept picking up cocorite. Deep inside, I knew that he might be right.

Another day was passing, and the coast was nowhere in sight.

Adri flung a fistful of cocorite seeds high into the bush. A flock of red and green parrots flew off with startled screams.

"Fine, if you like standing here so much, then go ahead and stay!" I shouted, slamming off along the curve of the river.

He stormed after me with a face like thunder.

****

Hours later, we could barely keep walking. I had set a blistering pace and Adri had done his best to keep up. I'd made it a contest in my head. At first, with his longer legs, I couldn't outpace Adri by much. Then through sheer will, what my mum called "bad mind", I pulled ahead. Now I had a small, petty smile on my face as I turned around to see him hunched over, breathing in little hiccups of air.

I could practically see the look on my mum's face, her round lips pressed together, heavy with disappointment.

"You alright?" I asked Adri, swallowing my guilt.

"I'm fine," he said through gritted teeth.

He straightened up and took a shaky step forward.

"Wait," I said, "I'm tired... Let's rest for a minute."

He hesitated, then eased himself down to the ground.

"What time is it?" he mumbled, streaked with dirt and sweat.

I pushed through the screen of leaves at the edge of the river and looked up into the hazy sky. It was later than I'd hoped. Adri was right. We were never going to make it out before dark.

"Let's find a tree for the night," I said, trying to keep the panic from my voice.

We drank as much as we could from the river, then got going. The trees around us were too short and thin to offer protection from the Flesh-skinner. So, I led us in a parallel direction, away from the water, tying strips of my torn shirt to branches at eye level, so that we could find our way back in the morning. It was an old hunter's trick Da had taught me.

Thinking about him made me desperate to get home. I just wanted this nightmare to be over.

"You alright?" Adri asked quietly.

"I'm fine," I shot back, swallowing hard.

There was no time to cry. The Flesh-skinner didn't

care how I felt. As soon as it was dark, it would be on our trail.

I led us away from the river as fast as I could. Adri was lagging behind me, but there was nothing I could do. I couldn't take his arm or let him lean on me. That might throw me back into one of his memories at the worst possible time. So, we struggled through the branches, together and alone. To make matters worse, the forest had thickened around us. We could barely get through. With the help of my cutlass, we broke, bent, and pushed our way forward, but it took forever to get anywhere at all.

Finally, we burst through the trees into a wide, round clearing. A few large trees had fallen, some time ago it seemed, opening this space up to the sky. Their moss-covered trunks, twice as thick as me, lay on the ground. On the far side of the clearing was a tall, solid tree, with a thick curtain of hanging green leaves. Sunset was coming. That's where we'd have to spend the night.

"Over there," I said to Adri, pressing ahead.

He didn't respond. I turned back to see him picking at a clump of bushes on one side of the clearing. He was plucking something and putting it into his mouth.

I ran up to him. "What's that?"

He was chewing a mouthful of bright red berries, the dark juice staining his lips. I grabbed them from his hand. They were small and glistening, like rubies.

"There's enough for both of us!" he shouted at me with disgust.

"Stop eating them!" I yelled, but it was too late.

I lifted the berries in my palm and sniffed them. They had a faint, tar-like smell. I could hear birds screech and twitter all around, settling in for the night. Da's advice about these things rang in my head.

I cornered Adri. "Did you see any birds near these?"

There were no animals near the bushes at all. Even the insects seemed to be avoiding their sickly-sweet smell.

He looked at me with wide eyes, a tinge of fear around his mouth.

I stared at him intently. So far, he seemed fine. I looked at the bushes again. They were laden with shiny fruit. How had I missed them as I'd rushed past? I looked at Adri again. His face looked long and subdued, but there was a strange glint in his eye.

"Please Miss, may I 'ave some more?" he begged in his best Oliver Twist voice.

"Oh, so now you have jokes," I swallowed a smile.

He was fine. I swung on my heels and headed over to the tree on the other side of the clearing. We could spend the night there.

"Hey," Adri sighed. "There's still e... ee..."

I spun around to see his body stiffen, as his tongue searched in vain for the word.

"No," I begged, running toward him.

Before I could get there, he slid to the ground as though the bones had been snatched from his body. In a flash, I was on my knees next to him, rolling him onto his back. His eyes were closed. I bent my head down to his chest and grabbed his wrist, searching frantically for a pulse.

***

When I lifted my head, it broke the surface of the sea next to an overturned boat. I coughed up air and saltwater. The beach was a couple of lengths away. I could see the surf rush up to kiss the sand. I was back in Adri's memory, again.

"Dad!" I screamed in his voice, treading water, spinning in every direction. "Ma!"

I could feel Adri's panic on top of my own.

Suddenly, his parents bobbed to the surface in deeper water, far from the boat. His dad was swimming with one arm around his mother, who seemed to need help. I raced toward them, or at least Adri did. I could feel the strain in every one of his muscles, the burning in his chest. He was swimming as hard as he could towards his parents.

Then, they went under. Just like that. No noise.

It was like a hand had simply plucked them down beneath the surface of the sea. I could feel the blood hammer in Adri's temples. The word 'shark' kept playing over and over in my head. Stuck in his memory, I did what he had done. I looked around wildly for something, anything, to use in my defence. All I could see was his orange lifejacket, floating nearby like a bizarre fish. He grabbed it and kept swimming.

"Watch out!" I tried to say as he raced through the churning water, but I knew it was no use. He couldn't hear me or sense my presence. Besides, this was a memory. I couldn't change the past.

Adri was swimming as fast as he could, barely turning his face to breathe. I could feel his limbs ache. The saltwater burned his eyes and the back of his throat.

He was still a good distance away when his dad popped up near the spot where they'd disappeared, held waist-high above the water by some invisible force.

"Dad! Ma!" Adri screamed, swimming frantically.

Where was his mother?

His dad seemed to be struggling with something under the water, punching and jabbing at it with all his strength.

Wait. There she was! His mum launched out of the water near his dad like a superhero. She slammed and hit whatever was holding her husband. I noticed that the waves broke on the spot they were on, like there were large rocks under the water. My mind spun. Whatever had Adri's dad in its grip was huge.

I wanted to turn back, but Adri didn't stop.

"Lila, Adri! The beach. Now!" his dad shrieked, punching and grappling, the waves breaking over his chest and arms as the water churned with the force of whatever he was fighting.

When Adri's mum saw him swimming toward them, she screamed, "No! Go back!"

She fought harder to get his dad free. Adri kept racing toward them.

Still wrestling with whatever held him in the water, Adri's dad looked right at him.

"Go!" he shouted, and his voice was a plea.

Then both his parents were gone, yanked underwater, before he could even blink.

Adri's body went numb. His mind cracked open. He looked at the space where his parents had been. There, in the distance, something boiled and bubbled beneath the surface. It started snaking toward him.

"Ma! Dad!" He scanned the water for any sign of his parents.

Then he turned and sped for the shore.

***

I opened my eyes back in the forest clearing, surrounded by watchful trees. How long had the vision lasted? Clearly not very long. I was still kneeling on the leafy ground. Adri lay in front of me, his eyes wide and staring. I yanked my hands away. They burned with an invisible force. The vision had taken over like a light switch, flicking on at his touch. I shook, still tasting the salt of seawater under my tongue.

I couldn't stop seeing his parents' faces – how hard they'd fought with whatever was beneath the water, how much they'd screamed for Adri to get to safety.

Now his eyes were open, staring up at me from the forest floor. I was back, the memory was over, but everything was still wrong. Adri blinked up at me, but nothing else moved - neither his face, arms, nor legs. Those berries he'd eaten... I put my ear close to his nose and mouth. I watched his chest, careful not to touch him. His breathing was slow but steady. I wrapped my hands in what was left of my shirt and tried lifting his arms. They flopped to the ground like beached fish. The berries had paralysed him.

"Can you talk?" I asked.

He blinked hard once. No.

I rocked back on my heels, biting back tears. Adri was alive and awake, but all he could move was his eyelids. I tried to sit him up and he just slumped back to the ground, his eyes round with fear. He was still breathing, but if the berries were poisonous, they could still kill him. If they didn't, the Flesh-skinner would. That hit me like a ton of bricks. Adri couldn't move and night was falling.

146

I sat there motionless in the middle of the forest clearing. Beads of sweat broke out on my skin. With the makeshift protection of my shirt over my hands, I grabbed Adri under his arms and began pulling him toward the tree where we had planned to spend the night. I didn't get far. The ground was uneven and covered with tree trunks, rocks, roots, twigs and piles of leaves. I released him with a gasp. Even if I could get him to the base of the tree, how would I get him up to safety?

Adri's eyes bored into mine.

"I don't know," I said aloud.

I looked around for another place we could hide. Golden sunlight was giving way to dusk. We needed light... That was it! The blood pounded in my head. I could light a fire to ward off the beast. There was only one small problem: I had no matches. I searched madly for two flint-like stones and struck them together over a small pile of brush, but nothing happened. I tried again and again. There was a single spark, but it wouldn't catch. There wasn't much daylight left. I kept trying. Nothing. Furious, I shoved the stones into my pockets.

Adri squeezed his eyes shut, then opened them and stared at me.

"No. I won't leave you here."

I could only imagine how crazy I looked, talking to a motionless body. I looked around one more time. A massive tree trunk lay on the ground nearby. Maybe this could work instead. I dragged Adri toward it. He moved his eyes from side to side, trying to see what was happening. The trunk was covered with bright green moss, finger-like mushrooms and spreading patches of lichen. I bent down and peered inside. It was hollow, lined with damp wood and leaves. I picked up a severed branch and beat on the outside of the trunk, standing between it and Adri. Fat blue beetles scuttled out in protest. I took a deep breath. No snakes. Good.

I bent down and used the stick to clear out as much of the mulch as I could. The cavity smelled like wet earth and mould. I stood next to Adri, hesitating. I could feel him trying to catch my eye, but I didn't look at him. The light was almost gone. What was that smell? Was it the Flesh-skinner? I started to shake.

"Close your eyes," I said to Adri.

My face was wet. He looked at me for a moment, then did what I'd asked him to do. I spread dirt, mud and leaves all over his face, body and clothes.

Hopefully, they would help mask his scent. Drenched with sweat, I pushed and pulled his body into the hollow trunk of the tree. It seemed to take forever. My hands trembled as I grabbed up loose branches, small plants and armfuls of leaves. I arranged them at the open ends of the trunk and along its length, camouflaging it as best as I could.

Then I heard it. The high-pitched cry of the Flesh-skinner. It sounded close. I sprinted toward the tall tree on the other side of the clearing and scrambled up into its branches. I peered back out through its shivering veil of leaves. Adri's tree trunk lay on the ground, covered with bushes and leaves. Had I done enough to hide him? He must feel suffocated, buried alive.

I could hear the beast crashing through the forest. The sour taste of fear filled my mouth. I shrank back into the shelter of the tree, praying that the hanging leaves would hide me from view. I squinted through the thin spaces between the leaves. It was like putting my eye to a shifting keyhole. The trees on the other side of the clearing began to shake without a breeze. There was a pause, a terrifying stillness. The Flesh-skinner knew how to be quiet when stalking its prey.

Suddenly a huge head burst into the open, moonlight illuminating its terrible face. I was so stunned I couldn't breathe. My mind dipped and whirled. The more I stared, the less I understood. The creature in front of me was terrifying alright, but it wasn't the Flesh-skinner.

Chapter Twelve

HUNT

The creature curled out of the forest in the last light: rust-red armour covered with bristling hair like the fur of bees. The body kept coming, long and segmented, like a giant centipede. Its legs, striped with bands of nightmarish yellow, moved with a slow, threatening crawl. Those legs, more than I could count, were as sharp as spears. They pierced the earth on either side of its seemingly endless body. I recognized the long, curling shape. It was the creature I had seen across the dead valley days ago – the one that had sent Adri and I running for our lives.

Now I was seeing it up close, and it was far worse than I'd imagined. Every part of its body seemed to be covered in a series of hard, metallic shields. Out of a massive round head, two arched antennae swung from side to side, as if tasting the air. The claws on either side of its mouth opened and closed like giant forceps. In the place of a face, the creature had a curved shield marked with a deeply carved X. As darkness fell, the X on its head shone with a red light that stained the vegetation around it like blood.

The creature paused and turned its head from side to side. From what I could see, it had no eyes. Yet it moved without hesitation, using other senses instead of sight. I stiffened as it began to sift through the forest floor, digging its claws into piles of leaves. Maybe this was how it hunted – scaring small animals out of hiding, rooting them out of their underground homes.

Please don't let it find Adri, I prayed in silence, digging my nails into my palms. It was so close, pushing at the fallen trees with its plated head, rolling one back and forth with its claws. I should distract it, throw some fruit into the trees away from Adri, but I couldn't move. Instead, I watched the X's head bend down to one of the fallen trees then pull back with a jerk. My skin crawled as it prodded and tugged at one end of the hollow trunk.

In seconds, Adri was out in the open, drenched in a pool of red light. The X ran its antennae along his body, its dripping mouth just inches from his face.

I thought of screaming, shouting. The stones I'd found earlier were still in my pockets. I could take them out carefully and throw them as far as I could, to draw the creature away from him. Then what? There was nothing else I could do; no plan that didn't end badly for both of us. So, I just sat there, shaking, trying not to throw up. The X curled its tail over Adri's head. At the end of its tail was a stinger, like a long, fine syringe. My eyes burned with tears. I felt my mum and dad urging me to have courage. Do something. But I didn't move. I pictured being eaten alive. This was one fear I couldn't face.

The X tensed, ready to stab down with its stinger. Adri was still paralyzed, unable to fight or run. He couldn't even make a sound. I hoped, for his sake, that it would be quick. With a hiss, a shiny green gel came spurting out of the X's sting. The gel coated Adri from his neck down in something like a bright, translucent sleeping bag. As soon as the X had Adri cocooned, it rolled him up onto its back and set off away from the clearing. This time, it sacrificed stealth for speed, crashing through the undergrowth. I watched from my hiding place, until it was out of sight.

I sat there, hidden in the tree, for I don't know how long.

When daylight came, I was surprised. The birds mocked me with their happy chatter. I lowered myself painfully from the tree and landed heavily on my feet. Invisible animals moved in the forest beyond me, but none of them came near the clearing. The trees turned their backs on me and shook their heads. I had failed. To my sleep-deprived eyes, the clearing in front of me became a whirling black hole. I stared into it, and it stared back. My reflection shrank down to nothing. The black hole tugged at me and dragged me toward it. It sucked me in and spit me out on the other side. I blinked in the faint light. I was still in the clearing, but something had changed.

A flood of rage rushed through me. Adri was no saint either. He had left his own parents behind. He was just as guilty as I was, willing to do anything to survive. What would I tell my parents if I ever saw them again? I didn't have to explain myself to anyone. No one was even here. If I never told them what had happened, no one would ever know. A small voice whispered that if I hid this, I would have one more secret eating me up inside. I told it to shut up and leave me alone. Adri was already gone.

But what if he's still alive?

To tell the truth, in the end, it was guilt that moved my feet rather than courage. I could see the line of destruction left by the X that had taken Adri. I followed it into the trees.

It had left a clear trail, littered with forest fragments. Here and there, the trees were tinged with fluorescent green slime. I moved as quickly as I could. Every time I felt exhaustion about to take over, I thought of Adri's eyes, wide open and blinking in the cage of his face.

By the time I paused, the sun had crawled high above the trees. I was at the crooked edge of the forest. In front of me was a landscape unlike anything I had ever seen. A dry, stony plain was crowded with tall rocks stained red, ochre, yellow, white, and grey. They pointed up to the sky. A thin layer of mist settled over the feet of those rocks like a shroud. There was no green ahead; nothing growing that I could see – only the pillars shaped like fingers of mismatched sizes and lengths, pushing up from the ground.

I moved in among them. The rocks towered above me like ancient termite hills or pillars from an old, forgotten civilization.

I could only get in by passing through the narrow spaces between them. A faint trail of green slime showed me the direction in which Adri had been taken.

The air was damp. My skin was covered with a film of moisture. The mist was thin enough for me to see several feet ahead, but I couldn't see past the crowd of towers to whatever lay beyond. I moved from one misshapen pillar to the other, looking for the green stains that marked the X's path. I hid behind each tower, looking in all directions for the X. If I stumbled upon it suddenly, there would be no way out.

The mist swirled around my legs like tentacles, drawing me in. It settled thickly around my ankles, until I could no longer see my feet. Suddenly, there were no more patches of green slime to follow. I looked around me. There were no marks to be seen. I had no idea which way the X had gone. I would have to keep going through this labyrinth of rock to find it. I inched slowly toward the nearest tower.

Maybe, if I hadn't fallen into the gorge a few days earlier, I would've missed it. However, this time, an inner sense of danger kicked in. I was moving slowly enough to feel my left foot step out into nothing but air. I jerked my foot back onto solid ground. What was this? It couldn't be a chasm. The way ahead was still blocked by rock towers. I sat down on the ground and slid my foot forward, feeling the edge where the rock gave way to emptiness. I pulled my foot back. There on my sneakers, sticky and fluorescent, was the X's bright green gel. It had slithered down this hole, leaving behind its telltale sign.

As far as I knew, the X could be close underground, tightening around Adri like a snake, alert to any intruders. I sat down quietly at the edge of the hole, taking care not to slip. Then I eased myself in, guiding myself down with my feet and hands. The walls felt like rock, marked and grooved by time.

The tunnel widened as I kept going. Soon I was able to walk upright. I clung to the wall in darkness, alert to every sound. The air was warm. I was slickwith sweat. It was like crawling to the centre of the earth.

Finally, I saw a faint green light ahead. It grew stronger as I moved toward it. I thought about the X possibly lining the tunnel ahead of me, but there was no clattering of its sharp legs, no sound to indicate its presence. I forced myself to keep moving. The light was coming from the end of the tunnel up ahead, shielded by rocks shaped like a snapping maw. I crouched between them, peeking out.

Beyond the tunnel was a cavern with a towering ceiling. The floor and walls of the cavern were covered with bright green moss that gave off an eerie glow. The ceiling itself was riddled with small holes, letting in thin reeds of sunlight like messages from the outside world. It hit me that I might never see that light again.

Where was Adri? I could see right to the other end of the cavern and the X was nowhere in sight. I sneaked forward, trying not to slip on the thick carpet of moss. The air was muggy and close. As I held on to the wall, my fingers were coated with that strange fluorescent green. I was shocked to see that the floor ahead of me was full of large holes like Swiss cheese. I would have to ease around them, without falling into whatever lay below. From somewhere beneath me, I could hear a rhythmic clicking and whirring, like the inner workings of a giant clock. With those sounds came a sharp smell that I couldn't place.

I stood there, shaking. If Adri was being held below, this was my best chance to find him. I went down on my hands and knees and crept forward to the nearest cavity.

As I peeked past the smooth edge of the hole, an invisible hand clutched my throat. I stared down into what looked like a bunker that was about an acre in size, about three stories deep, with spiked steel walls, lit by large pits of fire.

The space was crawling with X. Their monstrous legs skittered up and down the room. It was as loud down there as a factory floor – the X made the clicking, whirring noises of machines. At first, they looked like nothing more than a brood of seething centipedes. Then I realized that there was order to their movements. They were passing chunks of rock from one to the other, tipping them into fiery pits in the ground. The rock was the same dark metallic red as the X themselves. It gave off a strong acidic smell.

I slid backward slightly, terrified of being seen. What on earth were they doing?

There was a fire pit almost right below me. As the rocks tipped in, they broke apart into thick molten lava. The heat rose up to my forehead and eyes.

It grew more intense as the pit glowed brighter. I jerked back just in time. A scalding gust of red steam shot up from the pit, almost as high as the ceiling above me. The room I was in felt like a sauna, but thankfully the heat dissipated somewhat, through the air-holes above me. Now I knew what those holes were for.

I had seen enough. If Adri was anywhere close, I had to find him soon. These caves and the strange world beneath them were terrifying. I threaded my way around the holes on all fours, keeping my distance from the spouts of steam that shot up at random intervals. By the time I made it to the other side, I was singed and exhausted.

I dragged myself into the tunnel beyond. After the threatening green glow of the room behind me, the darkness was almost welcome. I tried wiping my moss-stained fingers on the ground, but my hands and knees still lit up like glow-sticks. Great. The X would see me coming from a mile away. I stood up, held on to the wall and went forward slowly, moving carefully around each bend. The floor of the tunnel sloped upward. I wondered if it led above ground. The air was cool and had a clean, fresh smell. The darkness seemed lighter ahead.

I turned a corner to find myself standing under an arched opening, looking out into a cavern covered with outcrops of crystallized rock. Gleaming stalactites and stalagmites pointed from the ceiling and floor, sharp as dragon's teeth. Some of them met to form gnarled, beautiful pillars. Thin lances of light pierced through scattered holes in the ceiling. Minerals in the rock made everything glitter and shine. The rock glistened with a thin sheet of moisture. Other than the occasional drip of water, the cave was quiet.

I slipped from pillar to pillar, hiding as much as possible in the shadows behind outcrops of rock. The silence was like a creature waiting to pounce. All around me the rock had taken on fantastical shapes. Some of them seemed to laugh at me; others shouted a silent warning. A flash of white caught my eye. I spun toward it, shaking. There, to my left, was a circular mound of rock, a bit shorter than me, with a curved depression on top. That bowl was filled with translucent white balls, each one three or four times the size of my fist. They were luminous, glowing in the dim light. I moved toward them, as if under a spell.

Chapter Thirteen
CHASE

Curiosity pulled me closer, despite my fear. The balls were stacked like piles of fruit. Each one was the size of a volleyball. They were white, gel-like, glowing. I bent over to look at them more closely, then scrambled back. My legs shook. I squeezed a thin pillar to keep from falling.

Inside one of the glistening spheres, two black eyes like marbles rolled toward me. My heart raced in my chest. I tried to calm myself down. Each sphere held a curled-up creature. They were strangely cute, with perfectly round heads and caterpillar-like bodies, no ears or noses, but with black domed eyes and mouths shaped like a "U", as though they were smiling.

I looked around me slowly. Air rushed from my

mouth. The cavern held more rock mounds like this one, each one of them filled with larva-baby eggs.

I was in the X's nursery.

Goosebumps crawled across my skin. These creatures were so many times the size of ordinary larva. They weren't even close to the scale of insects you found in nature. Not even the Amazonian giant centipede could compare. Those centipedes grew to be as long as a ruler. Yet, despite their fearsome appearance, they were part of the balance of the forest.

The X were something different. They were twice as long as most cars.

Someone had been messing with these animals, changing them in major ways, pushing the forest further and further out of balance. How long before the effects spilled out into villages like Samaan Bay, or other places closer to home? Maybe they already had.

In the eggs, the larva-babies, as if sensing my presence, had all turned to face me. They stared at me from their round worlds. Instinctively, I pulled back from their gaze. I ducked down behind one of the nests just as I heard a clattering, clicking sound. Something was coming. As I crouched down behind one of the egg-holders, a massive X emerged from the tunnel. It paused in the archway. Razor-sharp mandibles and curved antennae turned from side to side. I held my breath and ordered myself not to scream.

I cowered as the X took a step into the cavern. It stopped again. Had it sensed my presence? At any moment, it might rush toward me.

As I tensed to run, the X slung a cocoon to the ground. It was Adri, with everything but his head covered by the neon green gel. My heart sank. His eyes were closed. He wasn't moving. I tried to breathe quietly while the X lifted one of its sharp claws and sliced open the sac that held him. It pulled the sticky material off of him. Adri lay damp and still on the rocky ground. My head dropped, eyes burning. I was too late.

"Yaaahhhrgh!"

With a blood-curdling yell, Adri's eyes sprang open. I nearly fell over. The X's head jerked backward. Its massive, forked jaws clicked together. The many, jointed legs moved with terrifying precision, reaching for Adri's prone body.

I shouted, "Hey, you there! Hey!"

I was standing next to one of the pillars, in full

view of Adri and the X. Both of them were frozen, looking at me. I was holding one of the X's eggs with both hands.

"Back away from him now, or else!" I shouted.

What was I thinking? Would this work?

I held the egg above my head, squeezing it lightly. Would I really crush it? I hoped that the X believed that I could. Its glowering head followed my every move. Then it reared back and gave an ear-splitting shriek.

"I will! I'll do it!" I shouted, backing away slowly.

Adri was sprawled on the floor, staring at me in shock.

"Get up!" I yelled at him, keeping my eyes on the X.

Other than the endlessly twitching antenna, it kept absolutely still. It could take Adri out with one jab of its long, pointed legs, or a stab of the giant stinger on its tail. I had to hope that the survival of even one of these eggs was important enough to keep the X at bay.

"Adri. Now!" I pleaded.

He wobbled to his feet and stumbled toward me. The X's mandibles quivered and twitched. I held the egg close to my chest. Thankfully, the outside of the egg was slightly sticky, making it easier to hold, but what happened now? We couldn't go right past the X. I'd seen another opening on the far side of the cave. I had no idea where it led, but it was our only chance.

"Get behind me and hold on to my shirt," I ordered Adri, hoping that my trips into his memory happened on skin contact only.

I was about to find out.

"Took you long enough," Adri quipped weakly. "By the way, I had that totally under control."

I couldn't help grinning, but I could feel him shaking next to me. He was groggy, unsteady on his feet, but he would have to lead us out while I kept my hands on the egg and eyes on the X.

"Quick! Over there!" I pointed to the other side of the cavern with my chin.

The X was still motionless, but I could hear clicking and clattering in the tunnels behind it, growing louder by the second. It had called for backup.

"Let's go! Now!" I yelled.

The X parted its mandibles slowly and clicked them together once, like metal doors slamming shut. How much of what I was saying did it understand?

Adri tugged on my shirt. I nearly cried with relief. Finally, we were mobile. And better yet, I wasn't trapped in one of his memories. I put one foot behind me, then the other. I would walk backward facing the X. Adri had to be my eyes on the way out.

"Don't do it!" I said sharply as the X inched forward.

My fingers tightened on the egg. The X held itself poised like a cobra about to strike. Adri moved faster, dragging on the back of my shirt. I quickened my pace so as not to fall. I could really hear them now. The roaring clatter and shrieks of the X coming through the tunnels we'd left behind. Soon there would be too many of them to keep at bay, even with an egg.

"Duck," Adri ordered hoarsely.

I did, bending forward at the waist, keeping my face raised and my eyes on the X. It hissed at me from the other side of the cave. Adri led me backward into a low tunnel off the cavern. We had no choice but to follow it. Where did it end? If it led us deeper into the X's labyrinth, it was game over for both of us.

My heart lifted slightly as my arms brushed against both walls of the tunnel. At least, it was too small for an X to follow us in. Neither Adri nor I could walk upright, only in single file, with him facing forward and me shuffling backward, guided by his tugs on the hem of my shirt. I could hear Adri breathe heavily as he walked, hunched over, trying not to crack his head on the low rock ceiling. I made sure not to knock into him.

With my head and shoulders bent to avoid the roof of the tunnel, my face was closer to the egg. Through the translucent casing, I could see the larva-baby inside, wriggling slightly and looking at me with its black dot eyes. I prayed that the egg casing and gel inside it were thick enough to keep the little creature safe.

The tunnel twisted and curved until I had no idea how far we were from the X's nursery. Gradually, the roof grew a few inches above Adri's head and the walls widened.

"Okay, you can let go now," I told Adri.

"Okay," he stammered, fingers shaking.

He released my shirt and, in the slightly wider space, I squeezed around to face his back. He was trembling, with patches of green slime over his clothes and hair. My stomach rolled. I could still see him being dragged away by the X as I hid, trying to save my own life.

I shook my head. No time for this. We had to keep going before we both ended up as food for the X.

"Let's go," I urged him, "now!"

We continued moving forward through the narrow rock passageway. The egg was a weight in my hands. Both my arms ached. I worried about the small life inside. At one point, the walls were so close and the tunnel so dark that I could only tell Adri was ahead of me by the sound of his breathing and feet.

After what felt like an eternity, the ground began to slope upward. I could see more clearly. I looked down at the egg in my hands. It seemed okay. There was a faint but growing light around us. The walls of the tunnel widened further, and the ceiling got gradually higher. There was another opening ahead. I could feel it, smell it. The air around us had changed. It smelt of leaves and sunlight, of the outside world. I bit back a sob, afraid to hope.

"Hey!" I protested.

Adri had stopped suddenly, and I crashed into him, almost dropping the egg. He was standing in an oval of light: the tunnel opening. It was just big enough for us to go through one by one.

"Come on, let's go!" I begged.

Sunlight and fresh air leaked around him, but Adri wouldn't move. He looked over his shoulder at me, terror coating his face. His complexion was grey, streaked with mud and traces of green slime.

"It's okay," I said in what I hoped was a brave voice, "we still have this."

I lifted the egg slightly.

Adri looked at the egg and the tiny creature inside of it in a daze. I thought about the X coming to find us.

"Move!" I shoved him.

He stumbled out of the tunnel and ran. I was right behind him. After the darkness of the caves, the light was almost blinding. I had to blink several times before my eyes cleared. We were outside at last, in a totally different place than the field of rock towers where I had first entered the X's caverns. There, ahead of us, down a short slope, was the forest, with tall trees drenched in the golden light of late afternoon.

We had no time to admire this place's beauty. We had to get as far away from here as we could. I clutched the egg more safely in both hands and ran into the shade of the trees. I could hear Adri trying to push through ahead of me. We didn't get far before I heard the screeching-metal cries of the X. The sound gave our tired legs strength. I clung to the egg as I ran. It had a springy texture, like the tapioca balls I had first tasted in boba tea with my parents years ago. Their faces flashed across my mind for the hundredth time: Mum, Da and I looking at each other, laughing and slurping the bubble tea through fat multicolored straws. It felt as if that life where my parents were happy together had belonged to someone else, and I was watching the movie on-screen.

Now, as Adri and I ran over tree roots and piles of damp leaves, it was all I could do not to drop the egg. The clicks of the X were getting closer, but I had to slow down to check on Adri who was staggering behind me now on rubbery legs. He couldn't go much farther. We plunged through the forest as fast as we could. There, ahead of us, through the branches, we could see patches of still, brown water.

We ran out of the trees and pulled up short on a muddy bank. We were on the edge of a huge lake – flat and bronze in the late light. Thin ripples slid across its surface. The far side of the water was lined with low trees. We could hear X breaking through the foliage not far behind us. There was nowhere else to go. We looked at one another. I put the egg gently down at the base of a tree, out of reach of the water.

"What are you doing?" Adri objected.

It was no good holding it hostage any longer. I prayed that the egg would make it back to the nursery safely.

"Come on!" I urged Adri through gritted teeth.

I yanked off my boots and socks and tied the laces at the back of my neck. Adri's silver swim shoes didn't need changing. He looked at me, drained. We could almost smell the X's rusty odour, feel their stabbing claws. We stepped into the water.

The edge of the lake was shallow, but I had no idea how deep it might get. Still, we didn't really have a choice. We had to take the chance. I looked at Adri's haggard face. The ordeal with the X was catching up with him fast. He'd need my help swimming across if it got deep. I could only hope that I had enough strength left.

The lake floor was rocky at first. The stones hurt my bare feet. Then the ground sloped downward gently and became muddy and smooth, as the water slowly deepened around us.

Soon we were a good way from shore, but the water only came up to our waists. I began to feel better. If it kept going like this, we could wade right across. The only problem was that the other side of the lake still looked just as far away as it had from the shore behind us. What if the X caught up with us? I looked behind me – no sign of them yet. Maybe we'd make it out of this after all.

As the sun began to set, the distant horizon of land and trees became a dark outline against the pink and orange sky. The best we could do was keeping going and walk as far out as possible, conserving energy in case we needed to swim.

The sound of splintering wood and metallic screeching on the shore behind us signalled the arrival of the X. I snapped my head around, terrified. Three of them were breaking through the tree line at the edge of the lake. They slashed the tree trunks with their claws, drawing up on their back legs and trampling branches in a rage. Adri and I sped up, dashing through the water as fast as we could, but our chances of outrunning them were slim.

I glanced behind us. For some reason, the X weren't coming any closer. They didn't set foot in the lake. Hope rustled through me like a breeze. Maybe they couldn't touch water... I spat out something between a laugh and a sob. Adri released a sharp sigh. He had realised the same thing. The water wasn't that deep, but the X weren't coming in. They were smashing through the trees in frustration, screeching like trains, but they were afraid of the water. Once we kept going across the lake, we'd be safe.

"Zo?" Adri's voice was thin and strange.

He must be as elated and exhausted as I was.

I could see his face in the last light, turning toward me with shock and fear. What was the problem? We were both still here – out where the X couldn't follow. Then I felt it too.

With each step, my feet sank deeper into the mud. It was becoming harder to move forward. The mud clung to my ankles, sucking them down. Every step became a major struggle. Soon, we could barely walk. It was like wading through hardening cement. Halfway across the lake, we ground to a stop. The water was as high as my waist. I tried to step forward but couldn't pry my feet up from the mud. I reached down into the water, trying to yank my legs free. Fighting only made it worse.

Adri stared at me with desperate eyes. We were stuck.

Chapter Fourteen

GRIP

Quicksand. Of course. Why not blood-sucking leeches, or a shower of hail? At this point, any disaster seemed possible.

We tried to get free, but the more we fought to pull our feet out of the muck, the more it sucked us down, until we were chest deep in water and sinking. Behind us, on the edge of the lake, the X gnashed their jaws in rage, snapped branches and slammed trees, but they kept out of the water. Clearly, they'd understood the danger before we did.

Now the water was up to Adri's chest and my shoulders. My head spun. There was so much I needed to tell him: about falling into his memories and his parents' struggle to save his life. I needed to tell him how sorry I was that I'd left him back at the clearing for the X to take him.

There wasn't much time. The water was up to my neck now. I looked around for a floating branch, anything that I could use as leverage, but there was nothing. Adri was so quiet. He seemed strangely at peace, staring out at the rising moon on the far side of the lake. Behind us, even the X had fallen silent.

"Adri..." I started.

He kept looking away from me as though I hadn't spoken. My face burned with a mix of guilt, hurt and resentment.

"Adri..." I said louder.

"Wait," he raised one hand.

"Wait on what? 'Til we drown? I need to tell you..."

The look on his face stopped me short. His lips fell open as he stared across the lake.

"Look!" he shouted, as the water came up to his neck.

I turned to see a piercing blue light on the far side of the lake. It grew quickly as it moved toward us. I stared at it, mesmerized. It moved from a speck to the size of a flashlight, then a lantern. Soon I could see that the light was mounted on the prow of a small boat speeding across the water. Adri pointed, stunned.

"Help!" I screamed. "Help!"

"Help!" He joined in.

The X shrieked on the shore behind us. The brackish water of the lake slipped into my throat and made me cough. The water was lapping at my mouth. Adri and I waved our arms in the air.

"Over here!"

The water covered my mouth completely as I sank deeper into the mud. I tilted my head back, trying to take some deep breaths. Adri did the same, but how long could we last?

Back on the shore, the X rumbled and screeched like hurtling trains. The closer the boat got, the louder they became. Even with my head tilted back, the water was inching up to my nose. Soon I'd be completely covered.

The small motorboat raced toward us. It was being steered by a woman. She was tall and powerfully built, with long braids that flashed in the blue light. She looked from us to the X, her face like carved stone.

"Come," she said, throwing a rope out to Adri.

He shook his head. "Her."

The woman looked at me with something like disdain. Half of my face was under water. I held my breath and tried to stay calm. Finally, she threw me the rope. I held on to it for dear life. How was this woman going to get us out of the mud on her own, without capsizing the boat? Somehow, she did. I felt a strong pull on the rope and, bit by bit, it drew my legs up out of the mud. As soon as my feet were free, I swam weakly toward her. She steadied the other side of the boat as I climbed aboard. I turned frantically back to Adri. The water was just below his eyes. I threw the rope back out to him. Now I could see that it was attached to a winch and pulley, cranked by the woman's strong arms.

Soon, Adri was in the boat as well, panting and sucking in air, caked with mud and weeds. We all turned to look at the X on the bank. The noise they made was unbearable. Their sharp legs splintered the trees at the edge of the lake. The woman called out to them in a mocking tone, saying something that I didn't understand. The X stopped cold. The lights on their heads blazed to an almost blinding red, then dimmed until they were nothing but a soft menacing glow. I stared in disbelief as they turned and crawled back into the dark of the forest.

The woman laughed. Her voice was high and sweet like the twitter of birds. What had she told the X? Whatever it was, they had obeyed. Maybe they hadn't dared to not to. Even though she was dressed in a simple cotton dress and woven sandals, this woman carried herself like royalty. Her skin was dark and smooth as moth's wings. She was bare-armed, with knee-length microbraids laced with tiny silver beads. Her black eyes, lined with blue kohl, flashed like sharpened steel. It was clear that she was not one to mess with.

We were in a flat-bottomed wooden boat, with a motor at the back, three planks as seats and two long wooden oars. The woman began steering us to the other side of the lake. The passage across the lake felt like a dream. Blue light from the lantern, a small globe that hung from the prow, bathed the boat, forming a shield of neon light that moved with us across the surface of the lake.

Adri was sprawled on one of the low wooden benches that ran across the width of the boat, barely able to lift his head. I was in the same state. My legs were coated with layers of mud, still weighed down by the feeling of being slowly sucked into the earth. Something between relief and hysterical laughter burst from my mouth. Adri's eyes slowly regained focus. He stared at our rescuer. She was guiding the boat smoothly and quickly over the lake, her face intense, eyebrows set in a slight frown.

Who on earth was this woman? At least she had saved us from the X. But where was she taking us? I looked back over the water. The side of the lake where we'd run from the X was nothing but a dark band against the starlit sky. We had already reached the other shore. It was covered with thick mangrove swamp. I smelled the water, a funky blend of river and sea, with a hint of sulphur in it, like rotten eggs.

"Who are you?" I asked.

My voice sounded weak and shrill to my ears. Adri stirred but looked too worn out to speak. The woman ignored me, as she deftly guided the boat through what looked like a wall of dense vegetation. It turned out to be a carefully hidden entrance to a slow-moving river running through the swamp. The blue light bounced off the opaque water, the mangroves' tangled roots, and the thick dark leaves all around us.

I had come to a place like this with Da – the bird sanctuary in central Trinidad known as the Caroni Swamp. My mind raced. This couldn't be Caroni... That was on the other side of the island from Samaan Bay. I tried to think. Maybe we were in Nariva

Swamp – a huge area on the east coast of the island – but even that was shockingly far from the village. I didn't know how long we had walked through the forest and through those tunnels claimed by the X. How had we gotten so far off course?

"My name is Yara," the woman said finally, turning the motor down to a gentle purr and guiding us downriver with one of the oars.

She did not ask our names. Instead, she looked at me with eyes that seemed to judge and find me wanting. At this point, I didn't care. We had more important problems to solve.

"Do you know where Samaan Bay is?" I burst out. The words tumbled out of me in a mad rush. "We're lost and need to..."

"Samaan Bay is very far away," Yara interrupted me softly.

Her accent was different from anything I'd heard before. It was like a mix between French, Spanish, and a language I didn't recognize, with soft 's's and throaty 'r's. She sounded like a Haitian singer my mum used to listen to in the months before her and Da's divorce. Mum used to say that the singer's voice sounded like heartbreak and hope wrapped up in one.

I wanted to ask Yara where she was from, but she didn't look like someone who'd take kindly to personal questions.

I tried to focus on the matter at hand.

"Okay, but where are we now," I wondered. "Nariva?"

"Close," she nodded, without taking her eyes off the river.

My head spun. It was like we'd fallen into another world. Everything that had happened in the last few days came down on me like a flood. I looked at Adri. He seemed as overwhelmed as I was. Maybe that was why he was so quiet. I was tired of being the only one asking questions. Didn't he want to know where this woman was taking us?

I noticed that he kept stealing glances at Yara, then looking away every time her eyes happened to pass over him. Was he scared of her... shy?

A strange feeling twisted my stomach. Yara had a long striking face, fiery eyes, full lips, and thick eyebrows that almost met above the bridge of her flared nose. Anyone could see that she was stunning, in a warrior-princess kind of way. Maybe that's why Adri was so dumbstruck.

I rolled my eyes and snorted quietly. Boys. We'd

nearly died. Besides, she was way too old for him.

Speaking of old, it was tough to tell Yara's age. She'd hauled us into the boat with strength and ease. Her arms were those of a young woman, but at times deeper lines appeared at the corners of her mouth and eyes. They made her seem older. Still, everything about her had an air of elegance and mystery. I felt like a little kid in comparison. I could see why Adri kept looking at her, but it was irritating. I stared down at my mud-caked calves, trying to calm down.

As if he finally remembered that he could talk, Adri blurted out, "I'm Zo and she's Adri. I mean... Switch that..." he blushed and stammered, "t-thanks for getting us out of the lake."

"Yes... but how did you know we were there?" I wondered out loud.

Yara's smile was brief, like a queen dismissing her subjects.

"You are more than welcome... The creatures chasing you, they were not quiet. I followed the noise."

She spoke a bit strangely, formally really, like we had met at a grand ball instead of a lake full of quicksand.

"I too," Yara continued, "have survived the X."

Her fiery eyes were fixed on Adri's. He blushed and looked down at his shoes. I looked from Adri's red face to her expressive one, a bitter taste filling my mouth. No wonder Yara hadn't acted surprised to see those bizarre creatures. However, as far as I was concerned, what she knew about the X could wait.

I cleared my throat, "Miss Yara, thank you for rescuing us. Do you have a phone that...?"

Yara shook her head gently.

Of course she didn't. You probably couldn't even get reception out here.

"Well Miss Yara, would you be so kind as to take us to the nearest village?" I asked politely, holding back my "right now please".

From any village, we could get out of this nightmare and never have to see the X again.

Yara looked away from me to scan the swamp on either side of the boat. "Please call me Yara. I am taking you to shelter now. There will be time for questions and contact later, in safety."

I shivered. As much as I hated to admit it, Yara was right. We needed food and rest, but more than anything, we needed somewhere to hide before the night grew darker and the Flesh-skinner came hunting.

"Let me help," Adri offered, getting up and reaching for the oar in Yara's hands.

Yara smiled. "Thank you," she murmured, "but save your strength."

"No, thank you," I said loudly, "for everything."

Yara inclined her head slightly. "Shh now. There are other things in this forest besides the X; it would be best for us not to meet them."

So, she knew about the creatures. Did she know about the Zoo, the experiments? How much did she know? I tried to settle down but couldn't get comfortable on the wooden slats of the boat. It was better for me to stay alert anyway. The truth was, as grateful as I was to her for saving our lives, this woman brought more questions than answers. Who was she and what was she doing out here in the middle of the swamp by herself?

"Do you live out here?" I wondered.

Yara simply put one finger on her lips and looked around warily at the dark bushes on either side of the river.

Adri gave me a look that said, "Please chill." Then he hunched over on his bench, staring out at the swamp, as if he too were on watch.

I tried to read his face. Was he angry at me for

leaving him back at the clearing, for not even trying to find a way to distract the X before it took him? I felt a surge of shame that I buried with irritation. If he hadn't eaten those berries, we would be on our way to the coast by now, not here with some strange woman. Then an image of his limp body being dragged away by the X hit me. I swallowed a wave of nausea. These past few days had been beyond belief and the sooner they were over, the better.

As we slid deeper into the mangrove, my spirits lifted slightly. Mangrove meant that the sea was nearby, possibly right on the other side of this swamp. In the morning, with our new guide, we could get to the coast and on the road back to our families.

Well, my family... At some point soon, I would have to tell Adri the hard truth about his parents. I thought about them and the sacrifice they had made – a sacrifice that he couldn't even remember. Maybe, for now, it was better that way. The last memory I'd seen played over and over in my head, tormenting me. Their cries for him to get to safety; the horror he'd felt when they disappeared beneath the waves. Yes, he needed to know the truth soon, but it was so painful. This wasn't the time or the place.

The water of the river in the swamp was so dark that I couldn't tell how deep it was. I wondered if this was the lower course of the same river in which Adri and I had nearly drowned, ages ago. I rubbed my hands over my face. I didn't want to think about the past few days anymore, about the things that we had barely survived.

I tried to distract myself by identifying the different types of mangrove in the moonlight, the way Da had taught me. Here was the red mangrove, standing on roots above the water, grasping the riverbank like so many fingers. Over there was the black mangrove, with its roots sticking up from the waterlogged ground like straws, looking for oxygen from the air. I gently moved aside the flat, waxy leaves that brushed against my face. They belonged to the white mangrove. If I got close enough, I could see crystals of salt like tiny gems on the dark green leaves.

Each type of mangrove had found a way to grow in water that could wax salt or fresh with the tide. They used what they could and shed what they didn't need.

"Adapt to survive" was the way Da put it.

Now that phrase played over and over in my head. My heart tightened as I blinked back tears.

I'd run away, hurt my family, been rude to my Mum and Jake who had done nothing but care for me, all while trying to fight the inevitable. My life had changed, whether I wanted it to or not. It was time for me to change with it.

In the light of the moon, a bright spot caught my eye. It was a green snake coiled in the crook of the mangrove overhanging the river. I shuddered to think about it falling into the boat, but it didn't even move. It would wake up to hunt later. The night had just begun.

The rotten-egg sulphur smell of the swamp drifted across the boat. Two days ago, I would have teased Adri, elbowing him in the ribs: "Who smelt it, dealt it!".

Now I looked at him stealing glances at Yara, who showed no interest in talking to either of us. Right now, he probably wouldn't get the joke.

I turned my back on them. Even oysters were better company. They stuck like flower petals to the mangrove roots, next to small, barnacle-like snails. Petite red fiddler crabs sparred with each other on the mudflats. They choreographed elaborate dances of love and war, picked up tiny balls of mud and passed them through their mouths, then collected them in piles for later use. They crawled sideways along the mangrove roots and waved their one-sided claws at each other in welcome and warning. A large blue crab disappeared into its hole in the mud bank nearby, too mature for such goings-on. My mouth watered thinking about curried crab and dumpling. Wasn't Adri hungry? It had been a long time since our last meal.

A gnarled log in the water opened its eyes, revealing itself to be a caiman that sank slowly out of sight, leaving behind a silent trail of bubbles. It was probably thinking about dinner too. Mangroves were nesting grounds for so many birds, animals, and fish. I had heard of people spotting the endangered manatee, or sea cows, in Nariva Swamp, but none of them rose now to look at me with their gentle, whiskered, grey snouts. The more the swamp was cleared, made a dumping ground, or a free-for-all for hunters, the less chance I'd ever have of seeing these mammals that some sailors had mistaken for mermaids.

I inched back from the side of the boat. I'd read that, in Florida, pythons and crocodiles escaped animal smugglers and careless pet owners, to hide and breed in the Everglades – putting the local species at risk. I wondered if anything like that had happened here and what other creatures hid beneath the surface of the water.

I jumped when Yara said; "Sleep now, we have a long way to go."

Further to go!

"Where are we going?" I asked, my voice rising.

"Zo..." Adri cut in, irritating me.

Didn't it seem like an important question to ask?

Yara looked at us with a reassuring smile, "To my home. It takes all night to get there, and the nearest village is beyond it. From that village you can make calls, speak to the authorities. Out here, no phones work. After my house, we must walk to the village on foot. It will be safer to do that in the morning."

Adri gave me a knowing look, like, 'Satisfied?'

I pretended not to see him. Still, I thought about the Flesh-skinner and where it could be at that exact moment. I had to agree that her plan greatly increased our chances of staying alive.

"Sleep now if you can," Yara offered.

I shook my head. Thanks, but no thanks. I couldn't imagine falling asleep on the hard, wooden benches of this woman's boat, going who knows where. Adri yawned and lay down. He obviously had no such issues. His yawning made me yawn too. To say that I was extremely tired was putting it mildly. This had been one of the longest days of my life. But it would be over soon. All I had to do now was stay awake.

Before I knew it, my chin fell forward onto my chest.

Chapter Fifteen
WELCOME

"We're here!" Yara sang out.

Here where? I opened my eyes slowly. It was daylight. I had slept the night away.

Adri was stretching and rubbing his eyes on the bench behind mine. He had clearly done the same.

Yara was easing the boat up to an unobtrusive wooden post, stuck deep into the mud on the side of the river. She tied the rope to the post, took the now lightless globe from the front of the boat, and leapt lightly onto the bank. We scrambled out after her. With one of her rare smiles, she led us through a cunningly hidden gap in the mangrove.

"Follow me closely," she warned.

We walked behind her on an invisible track curving through dense hanging roots and leaves.

After a few minutes, I was more on edge than when we'd started. The air was hot and still. Mosquitoes dive-bombed my face and arms. My heart tried to escape my chest every time the undergrowth rustled. And then there was Adri... I could see him flinch at every sound too, then try to act like he wasn't bothered. If this was for Yara's benefit, it was pointless. She had looked back exactly once to check our progress. After that, she kept moving ahead at top speed. I scurried after her, trying to keep up. Adri had better do the same.

Finally, in what felt like the heart of the swamp, we came to a wall of some overgrown, creeping plant. I looked up and my mouth fell open in shock. The wall was part of a towering dome made from a finely woven trellis, overgrown with thick vines.

"Ouch!" Adri winced, holding his hand.

Yara turned to him. "Watch out. Thorns."

I wondered if I looked as bad as Adri did right now. The lower half of his body was caked in dried mud. His clothes were damp, green, and swampy. He smelled of sulphur-water and sweat. At that moment, however, he seemed totally unaware of his condition. Yara was fiddling with some part of the wall ahead of us. I tried to catch his eye, but all his focus was on Yara, as if her every action were pure gold. He seemed fascinated by this woman. I didn't care. If he wanted to be an awestruck little boy, so be it.

Yara turned to us with a triumphant smile. She had unlocked a low, narrow opening in the dome. We had to bend our heads to enter.

"Welcome to my home," she said in her musical voice. "Please, come in."

I pushed ahead of Adri. He could stand around staring at Yara. I wanted to see where this woman had brought us.

I was stunned.

Within the dome, the swamp disappeared. In its place was a lush garden, exploding with colour and the fragrant scent of flowers and herbs. Yara seemed to know all the plants' names and uses. She rattled them off as we walked by.

"Purple vervain to heal wounds and ward off venomous snakes. Bois cano for fever. Soursop leaves for sleep. Vetivier to calm the mind. Coconut oil for skin and hair. Good for cooking too. Shining bush to clear the eyes. Neem, Noni, Anamu..."

She sang their names. I floated through the garden in amazement. How had Yara made a haven like this in the middle of the swamp? Blue and orange butterflies flapped languidly through the air. Multicoloured birds chatted away in fruit trees of every kind. My mouth watered. There were tart green pommecytheres, sweet brown sapodillas, red pomeracs pecked white by the birds, yellow guavas with pink insides, soursop splitting open white and milky from their green horned skins, fat orange ovals of pawpaw and a towering chennette tree that would have made a good hiding place from the Flesh-skinner.

On its own, away from the other plants, I saw a silk cotton tree. Its roots ran over each other like interlocking snakes, weaving up the thick spiked trunk. Its branches reached out to the winds. I thought for a moment about Ms. K's stories of ancient spirits living in the silk cotton tree. Terrible things happened to the people who disturbed those trees, at least in stories. Here, it looked pretty harmless.

A path lined with orange and gold marigolds led to a neat wooden house, standing on stilts that raised it above the ground. To the left, a good distance away from the house, was a tiny shed that looked like an outdoor toilet. According to my dad's stories, it would be no fun to use that later.

To the right of the path was a cream-colored dome on a stone base, standing a bit taller than me, with a small arched opening. It was an outdoor clay oven. The last one I had seen was in a picture at the National Museum. Had Yara built all of this by herself? Impossible. She must have had a whole team to help her create this place. Where were they now?

"Greenheart. Termite-proof," Yara said proudly, pointing to her house. The stairs led up to a small, breezy verandah, but instead of taking us to the house, she led us round the back to a square stone structure with no roof and two swinging pine doors.

"I live simply," Yara said wryly, taking in my confused looks. "Soak the muddy clothes here." She pointed to soapy water filling a wooden trough. "Bathe now, then we eat."

She handed each of us a coarsely woven tunic, with a slight bow of her head.

"Thank you," I said.

"With deepest thanks!" Adri bowed from the waist, as if we were in a banquet hall.

I rolled my eyes and went in through the swinging doors. They led to a bathing area, divided in two by a tall, bamboo partition. I went left and Adri went to the other side. The floor was tiled with thick flat stones. On one stone, there was a slice of homemade soap that smelled of lemongrass and ginger. Next to it was a wooden bucket of water, and half of a dried calabash to use as a dipper. I sighed in relief as the sun-warmed water washed over me. I used my fingers to scrape the caked mud off my calves and feet.

"Zo!" Adri hissed across the wall between our bathing spaces.

"What?" I answered sharply.

He'd barely said a word to me since Yara appeared. Now he wanted to talk?

"Isn't Yara..." he whispered.

Great, he wanted to talk about Yara.

"Look Adri..." I cut him off.

I really couldn't take this right now.

"Is everything okay?" Yara's singsong voice wafted past the wooden doors.

"Yes, thank you!" I answered for both of us, grateful for the interruption.

After that, I heard nothing but water falling on stone. I finished bathing and dressing in silence. Adri didn't try to speak to me again and I didn't want him to. He was behaving like a lovestruck schoolboy. I came out to see Yara standing next to him, as he stood in his ill-fitting tunic. He looked stiff and embarrassed by her closeness.

"Good. Breakfast is ready," Yara trilled. "You must be hungry."

At the word 'hungry', my stomach groaned. I nearly tripped over my own feet getting up the stairs to the verandah. Yara hung our washed clothes out to dry in the sun. It was time to eat. Then as soon as our clothes were dry, we would go to the nearest village and call my family.

We went through the carved front door. The inside of the cottage was just as well-kept as the outside. We were in a simple, one-room kitchen with a seating area. There was an open window with a coal pot under it, next to a sink set in a long wooden counter. Beneath the counter was a large wooden basin that I assumed was full of water. Filling the rest of the room were a handmade table and four chairs. Yara directed us to them.

"Please rest," she insisted, with each attempt Adri made to get up and help.

She lit the coal stove, cracked eggs, and pulled delicious-smelling containers out of the cupboards. Soon, we had before us steaming wooden plates of warm coconut bake, fluffy scrambled eggs, fried bitter caraille and an assortment of homemade jams and chutneys made from fruit in the garden. To top it all off, we drank cups of yellow passion-fruit juice that puckered my lips with that perfect blend of tart and sweet. As I devoured my second serving of food, I noticed that Adri was barely eating. He looked drawn and sick.

I eyed him anxiously. "Hey, you okay? He ate poisoned berries a while ago," I explained to Yara.

"I'm fine," Adri snapped, embarrassed, as if I hadn't just said the truth.

I kept going, ignoring his red face. "He was completely paralysed, you know.

Couldn't move. That's how the X got us."

"Us...? Me!" Adri blurted out. He trailed off, looking away from me.

I avoided eye contact with him as well. Let him try impressing Yara with that story.

"Ah yes," Yara's eyes narrowed with concern as she took in Adri's pinched face, "how unlucky you were to find those berries. There are hardly any left in these woods."

"Drink this," she said, lifting a large green coconut, "it will help.'

She took a handmade cutlass from the corner of the kitchen, and with a few expert chops, cut off both ends of the shell. On one side, she opened the shell more fully and dug a hole in the exposed white flesh of the coconut, letting a little of the clear water spill out. She handed the first one to me. I threw back my head, swallowing the refreshing water in gulps.

Yara laughed approvingly, opened another coconut, and passed it to Adri. He took a quick sip, then set the coconut down.

When she started to clear the table, Adri jumped up to help her again.

"No, sit, please," she insisted, "it is not often that I have guests."

"But you still have to eat," Adri pointed out.

I felt a flush of irritation. He was so concerned about Yara. He should worry about us getting home.

"So, tell me Zo," Yara smiled at me from her place at the sink, "what brought you here?"

Adri's face tensed. I guessed he wanted to be the one to tell our story, but what could he say? He was missing an entire chunk of his memory. I hesitated, not sure how much to trust this woman. Still, she had saved our lives. So, I told her about being chased by the Flesh-skinner, getting lost in the forest, and finding Adri. I left out the part about Ms. K and spiders, remembering their warning. Then I paused for Adri to tell his part of the story. When he said nothing, I said that he had gone missing with his family and lost his memory. I told Yara about the X taking him. I skipped over my fear and doubt about whether to follow him and told her instead about tracking him to the labyrinth of rock pillars and the caverns below. I told her about the nursery and our close escape from the X's caves.

"A nest? Eggs!" Yara shouted, her eyebrows drawn low over her eyes.

"Well, yes... but what are those things – the X?" I asked, shuddering at the thought of their long bodies and scrabbling legs.

"You have seen them," Yara smiled thinly, "is that not enough?"

"And you have survived them, yes, even more fortunate," she muttered as if to herself.

"You said that you survived them too," I reminded her, "how?"

Yara gave me a fierce look, but when she spoke her voice was soft.

"It is amazing that you have made it here alive. Isn't

it, Mr... Adri?" she said turning slowly to face him.

"Adri?" This time I stared at him with real concern.

He looked sick. His head was bent forward, propped up on the table with both hands. I couldn't see his eyes. Maybe he was just tired. I was too.

"It has been a lot, yes?" Yara went on quietly.

"How did you fall into the river?' she asked Adri suddenly, her head cocked to one side like a bird.

His eyes fluttered open. "I...I...don't remember," he mumbled.

I interrupted. "Can we talk more on the way to the village?"

We needed to get home.

"Ah, yes," Yara continued smoothly, still focused on Adri. "Your parents. You do not know what happened to them."

Adri stared down at the empty table. What was wrong with this woman? Why go on about something so sensitive? I should never have shared any of this with her.

"We..." I tried to cut in, but she kept going.

"Why so quiet Adri?" Yara's voice grew softer, more sibilant.

I stared at her, disturbed.

"I don't remember," Adri answered in a strained voice.

Were those tears in his eyes? He didn't look up. One of his hands dropped, defeated, to the table.

"It must be hard for you both to be so far from home," Yara's words sounded kind, but her smile became harder and more fixed. Her teeth glinted in the light from the kitchen window. A chill ran down my back. Her face glowed as if by the heat of a fire. She swung around to face me with eyes like lit coals.

"And Little Miss Zo... Is that your real name? Two children, after all this time, who just happen to bring the X right to my doorstep...!"

She grew louder with each word. "Have you been sent to check my readiness, my loyalty? After everything we've done for the Council! They keep us in the dark about why you are here. Yet we must risk our lives to keep you safe!"

"What Council?" I whispered.

Were they the 'Bosses' Cap'n Peg had warned us about? The Council who started the Zoo – were they still around, running things in secret?

"Don't pretend to be ignorant," Yara hissed in my face, "you must know something... I am tired of being lied to."

She turned aside, muttering, "First, the Council asks us to keep the X under control. Now, you are sent. Why?"

"We're lost..." I tried to say, "we don't..."

"Lies!" Yara screamed. "While I was away with the one piece of armour the Council allows us, culling the X as they commanded, they sent my Kala to retrieve you on her own. Then they have the nerve to say she failed them! How could she do better with a few hours each night, after fighting through the X at every turn?"

Sent by the Council to retrieve us? Was this Kala the Flesh-skinner? I shook uncontrollably. We had to get out of here, now.

"Adri!" I pleaded, but he wouldn't raise his head.

Was he fainting? My stomach began to churn.

"And does the Council do anything to stop the X when they attack us?" Yara rumbled on. "No. For them everything is a test, and 'only the strong survive'."

She pulled herself up to her full height. "Well, we have survived. As have you..." she turned from me to Adri with flashing eyes. "Speak! Tell me what is at play! What is your role in all of this?"

I stared at her blankly. Adri didn't move. Losing

his parents, being chased by the Flesh-skinner, talking spiders, kidnapped by the X, and now this. He was going into shock.

"You think that the Council cares about you, about us?" Yara insisted. "Do you know why they didn't trust the X to bring you in? Those metal insects would have shredded you to pieces if I hadn't come along. Unless..." she paused, growing suddenly calm, "you are not the victims you appear to be. Perhaps, you work for the Council as well. Spies!"

"We don't work for the Council, or anyone else! We don't know what you're talking about!" I yelled, looking at Adri for help.

He didn't even lift his head.

"Okay, I will play along," her voice dropped suddenly, as if she had never been shouting, "come girl, tell me what you know, and you can go tell them that I passed yet another test."

"What are you talking about?" My head spun like a top.

Yara leaned right into my face. "Speak child, or else..." She smelled of ash and smoke.

Adri looked up and said quietly but firmly, "Leave her alone."

He spoke! Before I could say a word, Yara stuck a knife into the table in the place where Adri's hand had been. It was a miracle that he'd pulled his arm back in time. I tried to stand, then realised that I couldn't move. I felt weak, lightheaded. I tried to speak up, but my lips just bounced against each other uselessly. Maybe she had put something in our food.

Yara laughed sweetly.

"You are a smart one, Adri. And you care about the girl, yes? That may be of some use."

She brought her face right down to his. Adri didn't move or flinch. How was he being so brave? Maybe after everything he'd been through with the X, he'd decided to never be that scared again.

Yara smiled, her teeth sharp and glinting. "Keep you secure until further instructions. Those are their orders. Yes, I will keep you here, but you will answer my questions, or you might not enjoy the rest of your stay."

The word 'stay' was a low growl in her throat.

Slowly, Adri raised his eyes to Yara's burning gaze.

"You don't scare us," he said softly.

She does, I wanted to say.

Yara's expression made the hairs rise on the back of my neck. She was like a creature of wings, shadow and fire.

"Well then," she slapped her palms together like a door slamming shut, "stay you will."

Her eyes burned into Adri, then me, full of hunger and rage.

Under the table, Adri reached out and squeezed my limp hand. His fingers were warm and dry. I wanted to turn to him, to share in his spectacular calm, but I couldn't rip my eyes away from Yara's lightning smile. It was the last thing I saw before the dark.

Chapter Sixteen
SWING

I woke up with a throbbing pain at the back of my neck, surrounded by a horrible smell.

"No..." I groaned, wondering why my body felt so bent out of shape.

I opened my eyes to find myself staring at my chest and stomach. My legs were upside down, falling over my face. I was lying on my upper back with my neck cricked forward, my body forming an upside-down, lopsided 'U'. As I tried to right myself, the smell hit me again like a slap in the face. I broke out in a cold sweat.

I would know that smell anywhere. It was the rank, mouldy odour of the Flesh-skinner. I began to twist and turn as quietly as I could, trying to get into an upright position. Instead, I found myself pressed against some sort of woven mesh. A wave of vertigo hit me. I wasn't on solid ground. I was swinging gently from side to side, hanging in a net. As I tried to right myself, the swaying grew more intense. I breathed heavily, on the verge of throwing up, trapped like a fish on a line.

"Careful."

A wave of relief hit me. It was Adri's voice, speaking barely above a whisper.

"Try bending your right leg more, then the left. Okay, reach your hands up behind you and grab hold of the net. Now, try pulling yourself up."

I followed his instructions and ended up half-crouched, half-seated, but finally, thankfully, upright. My hands were gripping a hanging net of dried and woven vine, like the nests that cornbirds hung from trees. The gap in the weave was narrower than my arm, but wide enough for me to see through. There, to my left, was Adri, trapped in a net of his own. We were dangling between the rocky walls of what seemed like a deep well.

"Adri, the beast, it's..." I was on the verge of tears. The smell was all around me, choking me.

"Shhh," he whispered, pointing downwards.

I looked down slowly. Beneath us was a pit full

of darkness and foul smells. At its base, I could see the Flesh-skinner, lit by a few standing torches, surrounded by a pile of cracked bones. Its white skin was slick with phosphorescent slime, its huge head and jaws resting on its front feet. Its misshapen body expanded and contracted with each breath. It was sound asleep.

I fought the urge to vomit. My head reeled as the cave spun around me.

"Zo," I could barely hear Adri's whispers, but they were as calming as the sound of the surf in Samaan Bay, the place I'd refused to call home.

What I wouldn't give to be back there now.

"You trust me?" Adri asked.

The room righted itself slowly. I drew a hand across my face. It came back streaked with tears and dirt. Sitting in his gently swaying net, he pulled a small sharp knife out of his shoe.

"From the kitchen," he smiled.

I wasn't impressed. To the Flesh-skinner, that was nothing but a toothpick.

Adri pointed upward. A metal hook attached to a short length of thickly woven rope hung my net from the stone ceiling. His net was hung in the same way. There, in the ceiling between our two hooks, was a square wooden hatch like a trapdoor. If we could get to that door, maybe we could get out of here.

I looked down at the Flesh-skinner breathing loudly at the bottom of the pit.

"We'll fall," I moaned softly.

"No, we won't," Adri shook his head. "It's the only way."

He was already cutting into his net, slicing carefully to make a hole big enough for him to get through without splitting the net open and sending him sprawling into the pit below. When he was done, he looked at me.

"I'll throw it," he said.

"No." If I missed, and the knife went clattering down... "I'm not doing this."

There was no point. Where would we go once we got out? Who knew what else was waiting for us up there?

"You go," I said flatly.

"Stop it," Adri shook his head. "I'm not..."

"Leaving me the way I left you?" I smiled at him grimly.

I no longer cared. For me, it was over. Now, I just needed him to leave me alone.

"That night you couldn't move?" I admitted, staring straight at him. "I didn't even try to distract the X! I didn't even try."

"It wasn't your fault," Adri murmured through the gloom.

I wondered if, once he knew about his parents, he would be able to tell himself the same thing. It wasn't your fault Adri. Would he be able to live with himself knowing that he had left them behind, even if that's what they'd wanted?

Adri shook his head. "I'm not leaving you." His eyes shone in the half-light.

I never wanted to have to tell him what had happened to his parents. But I didn't want to live with it as my secret either, hanging around my neck. I was tired.

I looked down at the Flesh-skinner. After all the running, the things I feared most always seemed to find me.

"Do something for me," I asked Adri quietly, "when you make it back home."

He didn't answer. I could feel that he was already on his way out. He just needed a second to realize it.

"Tell my family... Mum, Da, Jake, Tayo. Tell them I'm sorry, and that I love them."

He was silent for what felt like a long time.

Then he sighed. "Okay."

I looked up at him. His face was a wooden mask. It was time for him to go.

He held on to the inside of his half-open net and braced himself against the mesh.

Then he swung toward me.

The impact slammed the air out of my body. I closed my eyes as the net swung through the air. I saw us both falling into the Flesh-skinner's open jaws. But when I opened my eyes, Adri was still there, holding on to my net with clenched fists.

"I would've warned you," he grinned, "but you were too busy giving your last will and testament."

A short laugh escaped my throat. I felt lightheaded. The metal hooks holding our nets to the ceiling creaked threateningly. Below, I could hear the Flesh-skinner begin to stir. We had troubled its sleep.

Quickly, Adri passed me the knife with one hand, while keeping a tight grip on my net with the other. I sliced as quickly as I could through the weave. The Flesh-skinner was snoring now. I could hear the crack of dried bones as its weight shifted in sleep. When the hole in my net was big enough, I slipped the knife back to Adri. He slid it into his pocket. He was still holding on to my net, looking at me.

"Are we going or what?" I grinned weakly.

When he smiled, it lit up his whole face.

He whispered "Now," and let go.

Even as my net swung away, I started climbing.

A huge roar shook the cave. The Flesh-skinner was awake.

I made sure not to look down, bracing myself with my hands and feet. The net swayed with every movement. I climbed up carefully, drawing on my years of gymnastics. One slip would send me tumbling into the Flesh-skinner's jaws. After what seemed like forever, I grabbed hold of the rope and hook holding the net to the ceiling. I looked across at Adri. He was moving more slowly up the weave of his net, stopping and holding on for dear life each time it swung and twisted through the air. His face was wet with the effort. Every inch of his body seemed focused on not falling.

From the sound of it, the Flesh-skinner was flinging itself against the sides of the pit, trying to scramble up to reach us. Finally, we were both just below the trapdoor.

"We'll have to hit it at the same time!" Adri shouted over the Flesh-skinner's howls.

I held on to my rope and hook with one hand, my feet jammed precariously into the weave of the net. Most likely, Yara had already heard all this noise. Once we got out of the pit, we'd have another fight on our hands. But, first things first.

Adri counted down, "One, two..."

On three, we slammed our fists into the wooden panel above us. It shuddered with the first blow. After the fourth, it flew open.

"Come on!" I urged Adri, trying to ignore the Flesh-skinner's screams.

I swung myself up and grabbed the edge of the opening with one hand. I took a deep breath, zoned out Adri's worried face and the sound of the Flesh-skinner growling beneath me. Then I let go of the rope and swung my left hand up to the edge of the trapdoor opening, as well. With all my strength, I pulled myself up by both arms, until my upper body was through the hole and onto the floor above.

I pulled myself to safety. My arms were shaking as I turned back to look for Adri. I could see one of his hands grab the edge of the opening, then slip as he lost hold.

I gasped and reached for him, but it was too late. Frozen, I lay just beyond the opening, listening for his screams. It was silent. I inched forward on my stomach, until my head and shoulders were over the pit. The Flesh-skinner was on its hind legs, driving its body up the sides of the cavern, spit flying from its massive teeth. Adri hung on to his net with one hand, his feet dangling just above the Flesh-skinner's jaws. I moved to climb down to him but caught a glimpse of the hook that held his net to the ceiling. It was coming loose. There was no way it would bear our joint weight.

"Come on, you can do this!" I shouted like a psychotic cheerleader.

My heart was racing, but there was nothing I could do. Adri grabbed the net with both hands and tried to pull himself higher up. The Flesh-skinner propelled itself up the rock wall, getting closer to his feet each time, until it was practically snapping at his toes.

Finally, Adri managed to get a foothold on the weave of the net. He started climbing back up.

"Hurry!" I screamed.

The hook that held his net in place was coming loose, fast. I wiped my damp hands on my pants again and again. He climbed frantically until he was clinging to the rope just below the opening. I could see the whites of his eyes and the beast snapping and spitting beneath him. He was too winded to speak. I reached out to pull him up, then jumped back as if I'd been yanked by an invisible hand.

"Zo!" he shouted, terrified.

I had forgotten the memories. They had always been activated by touch. All I wanted at that moment was to give him my hand and pull him to safety. But, if I fell into one of his memories, that one moment could be enough to send us both falling into the Flesh-skinner's jaws.

"Help!" Adri clung for his life to the rope at the top of the net. He stared at me confused and hurt, wondering why I wouldn't just grab his hand and pull him up. His eyes filled with angry tears.

"I can't," I groaned.

The tiny room around me was empty. There was nothing else I could give him to grab hold of. I inched toward him, then pulled back. I couldn't take the chance.

Adri's breath came in hard gulps. He gripped the edge of the opening with one hand, then the other. Slowly, excruciatingly, crying out in pain, he heaved his body up onto the wooden floor.

He lay there, swallowing air, staring at me with wide, betrayed eyes.

"I thought I was fainting. I was scared I'd drop you," I stammered, hoping that he would believe my lie.

The Flesh-skinner's rage rose to a deafening roar.

"The noise... Yara!" I rushed, trying to change focus. "We have to get out of here before she comes!"

We were in a small empty room, with wooden walls, one door and a high window that let in a wash of silver light. Yara hadn't even bothered to lock the door. I guess no one had escaped this way before. Shaking, we stumbled outside to find ourselves standing in front of the small blue shed that stood in Yara's richly scented yard.

It was nighttime. The garden was a blend of pale light and shadow, full of sinister shapes. The tall dome loomed over us. We hobbled along the path toward the cunningly hidden entrance that Yara had unlocked earlier. We'd have to find a way to open it ourselves.

Before we could reach it, a terrible sound reached our ears. Somewhere in the bowels of the earth, there was scraping stone, then we heard the pounding steps of the Flesh-skinner drawing closer.

I tried to drag Adri by his tunic towards the nearest tree, but there was no time. The Flesh-skinner was already racing toward us, green spit flying, snapping its long, ivory teeth.

Chapter Seventeen

FIGHT

The Flesh-skinner would finish us off in seconds. At least, I hoped it would be that quick. I closed my eyes, hearing Adri's ragged breathing. A loud crack split the sky above our heads. I looked up. There, high above us, biting furiously through the roof of the dome, was a giant X.

The Flesh-skinner skidded to a stop. It bayed loudly, stunned. There were eight or nine X crawling and slithering over the dome. They began smashing and gnawing their way through the thorny barrier. Shredded leaves, branches and lashing vines came crashing into the garden below.

I grabbed Adri again and pulled him behind a wall of hibiscus bushes nearby. The thick, tall hibiscus had been planted around a rock garden full of grey stones. All around us, red, yellow, pink, and purple flowers hung their heads, their petals closed for the night. We crouched behind the dense bushes, desperate for any kind of cover. So far, no X were crashing through the part of the dome directly above our heads. This little area wouldn't hide us for long, but it was the best we could do on short notice. Climbing trees wouldn't help us now.

Where was Yara? Strangely, even with all this commotion, she was nowhere to be seen.

I peered through the hibiscus branches and saw that the first X had already broken through the dome. It slithered down into the garden. Before it could hit the ground, the Flesh-skinner attacked. The X lashed the air, but the Flesh-skinner sank its fangs in deep, like a lion biting into a wildebeest. The Flesh-skinner roared in defiance as more X crawled in through cracks in the ripped dome.

Suddenly, the Flesh-skinner's howls turned to yelps of dismay, as it backed away from the advancing X. Adri and I looked at each other, confused. Why wasn't it fighting? Then I saw the angry sores breaking out on the Flesh-skinner's back.

"The sun!" Adri groaned.

Without us noticing, dawn had crept into the garden. The Flesh-skinner bayed in agony, as the sun's early rays bit into its unprotected skin. Two X closed in on the distracted beast, while the others pushed through ripped holes in the dome. Adri tapped my arm and signalled silently. The X were still focused on the Flesh-skinner. Now, we could escape. We crept out of the bushes and moved quietly toward the door that led out of the dome.

Before we could get close, the arched gateway slid open. We pulled up short. Yara appeared, blocking the way out. Her eyes burned and a crescent sword glinted in each hand. We were out in the open, exposed, but she acted as if we weren't even there.

She let out a high-pitched cry and ran furiously toward the Flesh-skinner. Thanks to the sun, it was writhing in pain, spiked head low, trying to keep the X at bay while sores spread all over its body. As it turned to ward off one X, another drew back its head, about to snap down on the Flesh-skinner's neck.

In a flash, Yara leapt through the air. Ahead of her, she flung the small blue globe that had lit our way the night before. She landed on the back of the X that was about to bite down and sent it rolling with one slice of her crescent swords. The blue sphere hit the Flesh-skinner's head and clicked open into points like a three-dimensional star. Then it expanded into panel after panel, covering every inch of the Flesh-skinner's body, protecting it from the painful sun. Meanwhile, Yara spun her swords furiously from side to side, warding off the X.

"Now!" I whispered, snapping back to my senses.

We turned to run out of the dome, but it was too late. An X was already there with its back to us, blocking the narrow doorway. Shaking, we dashed back to the hibiscus bushes and took cover, peeking through the web of branches.

The Flesh-skinner was covered in metallic blue armour now, shielding it from the sun. Together with Yara, it began to wreak havoc on the X. Two X lay on their backs with their legs in the air. The Flesh-skinner turned and slammed another with its armoured tail.

The remaining X dashed forward, chittering with rage. Yara leapt onto the Flesh-skinner's back and turned to face them. She held a white orb in one hand. The X froze.

"Yes! I have been to your home, as you have so kindly visited mine."

The X started toward her, then screeched to a stop as she gripped the ball tighter. When I realised what she was holding, my stomach flipped. Yara threw the white ball high in the air.

"Go home and look to your eggs!"

The Flesh-skinner opened its jaws wide and swallowed the egg with a single gulp.

Adri flinched next to me. I knelt there, stunned. Yara smiled triumphantly. I bent over clutching my ears as the X shrieked in pain.

When I looked up, Adri's face was full of horror. I soon saw why. Through the doorway and every crack in the dome, streamed tens of X. Their speed made them seem even greater in number. They were smaller in size than the others, about my height. The giant X's children. They twitched and chattered, clacked and screeched, with the sound of metal grating against metal.

Yara's face fell, then hardened. The Flesh-skinner groaned as the X rushed towards them like a wave. Yara flashed like lightning from place to place, slicing at the smaller X. She seemed to fly through the air, screaming defiance like a bird of prey. The Flesh-skinner danced at her side, crushing, biting and butting the X with its head, claws and tail.

But, soon it became clear that Yara and the Flesh-skinner were severely outnumbered. In seconds, they were cut off from each other. A circle of X closed in on Yara like a pack of wolves. One of the adult X slithered slowly toward her from behind, as she tried to keep the smaller ones at bay.

I opened my mouth to scream a warning.

"No!" Adri hissed, trying to grab my arm.

Behind Yara's back, the massive X was about to strike.

"Look out!" I yelled, dragging my arm out of Adri's reach and throwing a large stone at the X.

Just then, the Flesh-skinner knocked the massive X away from Yara.

"Oh no!" I cried.

My stone accidentally hit the Flesh-skinner in the head, knocking it off balance just long enough for a huge X to take hold. Yara kept fighting the other X, but they kept her from getting close enough to help the Flesh-skinner. The beast bayed as the giant X curled around its body, latching on to the Flesh-skinner's armour. They rolled over in a vice grip. With its huge mandibles and hundreds of prying legs, the X dug into the Flesh-skinner's armour, wrenching it up plate by plate.

That stone I'd thrown had only made things worse.

Yara spun like a whirlwind, fighting furiously to get to the Flesh-skinner. It scraped at the X, trying to break free. Just then, the X stabbed down with its sting. Even at that distance, I could see a bright green liquid shoot through the Flesh-skinner's pale skin. It fell, but kept its grip on the X until those centipede legs were still.

The exposed patches of the Flesh-skinner's skin sizzled in the sun. It whimpered in pain, struggled to get to its feet, and finally fell forward with a loud crash.

"Kala!" Yara screamed, carving a way to its side.

Kala... Kala was the Flesh-skinner's name. The one who'd been sent to "retrieve" us and failed. I shuddered, thinking about how we'd barely escaped, wondering if we'd get another chance to try.

A horde of the young X rushed toward the Flesh-skinner, Kala, to finish her off.

"Come on!" Adri begged, pulling me away.

I soon realised why. My shouts and stone-throwing had drawn the attention of several of the smaller X. They were quietly closing in on our hiding place. I looked around frantically. It was too late. With a loud cry, the X skittered toward us, their legs like hundreds of needles stabbing the dirt.

Suddenly, out of nowhere, I heard the faint sound of drums. The X skidded to a halt. Between them and us, something was appearing out of thin air.

"They're coming..." Adri muttered in shock.

"Who...?"

Then, I realized that the thing forming in front of us was a giant web.

Out of it stepped a towering spider, made of glass and metal, with creaking joints and spinning claws on the ends of its legs. It lumbered and swayed. The chittering X took several steps back. They seemed as unsure as we were about this new machine.

In the distance, Yara seemed to be defending Kala, while trying to get her to move to safety. I didn't have time to focus on their situation. We had problems of our own.

The web disappeared along with the whisper of drums. It left behind the Metal Spider, tall as a tree, flexing its legs while trying not to fall over.

"What on earth?" I whispered, turning to Adri.

A rock went whizzing past my head, smacking into the Metal Spider's stomach.

"Ay! Watch how you throwing stones, you rock-headed boy!"

I knew that voice! It was Cap'n Peg.

As the Metal Spider bent over us, I could see her sitting inside of its large glass head, pushing a joystick and working a set of controls. Eight other spiders were seated in a circle around her, each working frantically to manage one of the Metal Spider's legs.

No wonder it was almost falling over.

The X around us started twitching and creeping closer. Clearly, they weren't that impressed either.

"Watch out," Adri warned.

"Eh heh? You better listen to Cap'n!" A spider with an airman's cap and goggles shouted at us, waving her arms and letting go of the controls.

One of the Metal Spider's legs went limp. It staggered to one side.

"Hey Eyeballs!" a spider with a blue mohawk pointed out. "Watch what you doing, before you get us all killed!"

Shamefaced, Eyeballs grabbed the controls.

Adri and I looked at each other. Time to move.

We backed away as the X inched closer, their chatter growing louder with each step. In her corner, Yara was barely keeping the X off Kala.

Meanwhile, Cap'n Peg complained, "Piece ah

scrap metal! I don't know why these people never give us good things. Look at what these overgrown centipedes get!"

At that, the surrounding X screeched and raced forward, the X's on their heads flashing bright red with rage.

"Throw!" Adri screamed.

He was picking up the stones that decorated the rock garden and sending them flying into the rush of X. I did the same, but as many as we threw, the X kept coming. There were just too many of them.

"Attack!" Cap'n Peg roared.

The Metal Spider flailed its legs once, then twice, knocking X out of the way. Then it tripped over a stone and fell, swarmed by X trying to pry their way inside.

"You bow-legged landlubbers!" I could hear Cap'n Peg shriek, surrounded by a loud chorus of panicking spiders.

At any other time, it would've been funny, but right now we didn't have the time to laugh.

The X closed in on us, snapping their jaws. Their sharp stingers glinted in the light. Adri and I crept backward, but there was nowhere to go.

Suddenly, I heard a noise. It was oddly familiar,

but it wasn't the drums that played every time the spiders made their webs. It was a hum, growing louder and more insistent.

I realised that it was a sound I'd hoped to never to hear again. The X skating toward us heard it too and they skidded to a stop, looking behind them. Yara had one hand on the Flesh-skinner Kala's motionless head. Around them were the bodies of several X. Those that remained, including a few large X, closed in, careful to stay out of reach of her crescent swords. The smaller X who'd been scrambling toward Adri and I, rushed back to join them with terrifying speed.

Yet Yara just stood there, perfectly still, her face set like an ancient carving. In the heart of the chaos, she was singing a song in a language I didn't understand. The hum grew louder as her braids lifted into the air, stretching out around her in a stunning halo. The silver beads that lined her hair glittered in the sun. Adri and I stared motionless as the beads lifted off Yara's braids, leaving them to fall back down gently past her hips. Now, the beads were flying on their own. A silver cloud trembled above Yara's head. It was the swarm of gnats that had surrounded me on Rain-Tree Hill.

Their hum became a buzz, then a deafening roar. In a split second, the silver cloud glowed green, and the swarm descended on the X, sending them scattering.

"Adri, down!"

Before he could run, I pushed Adri to the ground and threw myself down next to him.

"Don't move," I warned him.

He did as he was told. From the ground, I looked in the direction of the gnats.

The swarm had broken into smaller clouds that fell on the X, disappearing like green smoke under their armour, while they reared and squirmed. The buzzing swarms re-emerged from the X's armour only when they fell, twitching, to the ground. I remembered the pain of those stings, how they had weakened every muscle in my body and put me to sleep. The X were getting a dose of that medicine and I was pretty sure they didn't like it.

"Come on, ladies! Time to go!" I heard Cap'n Peg shout, as the spiders tried frantically to get the Metal Spider on its feet.

In seconds, the gnats were on them like a whirlwind, zipping into the joints of the machine. I could hear the spiders slapping and fighting off the invaders for a few seconds. Then the Metal Spider just lay there, as the swarm of gnats slipped out, looking for their next victim.

My heart sank, but I didn't dare move to check on the spiders. I could hear Adri next to me, trying to breathe more quietly.

Across the torn-up garden, Yara urged Kala to get to her feet, trying to move towards a large gap that had been broken in the side of the dome. She removed any X that flailed into her path with one swipe of her swords. The swarm left them alone, but Kala kept slipping to the ground with each step. They had a long way to go before they could escape. I felt sorry for them, and for us.

Then a few large X started spraying green gel from their stingers into the clouds of insects, trapping them in thick clots of gel that fell out of the sky. Soon, only two of the largest X remained, but there were no gnats left.

While Adri and I stayed completely still, the X headed straight for Yara and Kala.

I felt like someone was choking me. Could Yara fight off the X and protect Kala at the same time? I looked at Adri. His face was grim.

"Let's go," he whispered.

"Wait," I pleaded.

"Why?" Fear and anger fought for room in his face.

I wasn't sure. Yara had locked us up, threatened us. Yet somehow, after the way she'd fought against the X, the way she and Kala had defended each other, it seemed wrong to leave them without even a witness to remember their fate.

Yara looked up at the approaching creatures with exhaustion and rage. Kala was barely moving. The two X limped toward her, then picked up speed, raising dust with their sharp claws. Yara stood up and flicked her crescent swords out with her wrists, until they became two long bronze sticks. She slammed one of the sticks into the ground by Kala's head and the other just beyond her spiked tail. There was a flash and, in an instant, both Yara and Kala were covered by a shell of blue light. The X were right over them, but they slammed into the blue light like a wall. They could not get through. It was some type of forcefield.

"Kala," Yara shouted, kneeling and holding the Flesh-skinner's face in her hands. "Gather your strength. We have to go."

Adri and I could see and hear them clearly. The forcefield stopped matter, not sound. The X flung themselves at the shield in a frenzy, slamming themselves against the blue shimmering wall.

Every part of me froze. The hair on my head stood on end.

I heard Kala, the creature I'd called the Flesh-skinner, say in a woman's low voice, "Yara, it is time."

Kala had talked... like a person.

Adri and I stared at each other in shock.

Kala's pale sides heaved, as she fought for breath. She looked at the X. They kept crashing into the forcefield. I could see lines appear across its blue surface like a cracked windshield. It could break any second and there would be nothing to stop the X's rage.

Yara rested her face on Kala's cheek, oblivious to the pink sores and green slime.

"No," she said, her voice breaking. "We can still make it... Please."

Kala coughed up red foam, her bare skin marked and broken by the sun.

She looked around. The shield was covered with more cracks than a turtle's shell. Her voice was hoarse, chest rattling.

I could barely hear her speak.

"It has been...long...enough. I am ready."

"No, no," Yara kept saying, her braids falling over Kala's side, while she caressed her massive head, face, and claws.

Pieces of the forcefield fell off like broken glass. The X gibbered and poked at the holes, trying to widen them enough to crawl inside. They were almost through. When they were finished with Kala and Yara, we'd be next.

Adri was pulling me now, dragging me towards the exit from the dome. I went with him, but I couldn't look away from the cracked forcefield, surrounded by lashing, relentless X.

Kala gazed at Yara with glowing eyes.

"Little sister," she said clearly, "go free."

Suddenly, red light filled her chest. It spread out to the blue forcefield, staining it purple. It crept toward the bronze posts stuck in the ground on either side of her body.

The posts, the forcefield, Yara's face and hands, all shone in the purple light. Then the light pulsed outward from Kala in a silent and powerful blast. I felt the energy rush over me like a crashing wave. Adri and I went rolling and sliding across the ground.

When I sat up, groaning, Adri was splayed next

to me, trying to get to his feet. I looked around in shock.

The dome had been blown open on all sides. Trees and bushes lay on the ground, uprooted. The house, the shed and bathing area were piles of rubble. Beyond the dome, the mangrove was flattened as far as my eyes could see. The remaining X were on their backs, completely still, heaped up like debris after a storm.

Yara knelt at the heart of the explosion, with her face buried in Kala's neck, her shoulders heaving with grief.

Adri and I struggled to our feet.

"Look," I stammered, pointing with a dirt-stained, trembling hand.

Before our eyes, the Flesh-skinner shimmered and changed. In its place was a petite young woman, with a big red afro, and Yara's stunning features under pale, freckled skin.

The creature I'd called a beast all this time was actually Yara's sister. She was more than the monster I'd seen. They'd risked their lives for each other, and Kala had given hers for the person she loved. Adri stood in stunned silence next to me. Beyond the shattered remains of the dome, in the flattened mangrove swamp, I could see the brown curve of the river not too far away.

We stumbled in that direction.

Yara didn't look up. She was sobbing hoarsely into Kala's peaceful face.

"Wait a second," Adri stopped.

I stood there, confused.

He went over to the Metal Spider. There was a wide crack in the machine's glass head. We could see the spiders jumbled inside.

"Are they...?" I mumbled.

"No," Adri reminded me, "tranquilized by the gnats' stings."

He pointed to Cap'n Peg's stomach that was gently moving in and out in sleep.

"Over there," he ordered, "pass me a vine and that branch."

I didn't have the strength to argue or ask why.

We stumbled out of the ruined garden, with Cap'n Peg strapped to a stick over Adri's shoulder, through what used to be a living world, home to so many plants and animals, creatures known and unknown. We walked until we could no longer hear Yara's cries.

Chapter Eighteen
TURN

Adri and I limped quickly along the damaged riverbank, through splintered bushes, hearing animals scuttle and hide. At least they'd survived the blast.

Now we had to get as far away as possible, before more X turned up, or worse.

I tried to make sense of what we'd seen and heard. The Council, the shadowy organisation that had started the Zoo, was still around. They'd only pretended to abandon the research centre years ago, probably to avoid unwanted attention. From the X to the spiders, and the Flesh-skinner Kala, they were clearly still experimenting on animals... and people. But what did they want with me and Adri?

Unlike research that tried to do some good in the world, the Council seemed to be all about twisting nature into weapons. Who knew how they planned to put those weapons to use? I looked around me carefully. Maybe they were watching us now. Maybe they'd been watching us all along. But if they were watching, why allow us to go free?

A cold line of sweat ran down my neck. Getting home might be even harder than I'd thought.

"Come on Zo, we need to move," Adri urged.

I tried to keep up, but my legs felt like jelly. Adri, on the other hand, had new energy. Being captured by an X and nearly eaten had clearly changed everything for him. He moved at top speed, while Cap'n Peg dangled from the branch on his shoulder. She was still out cold from the gnats' stings. If anyone could answer our questions, it would be her. I figured that was why Adri had brought her along.

I tried to keep up, distracted by the destruction around me. Mangrove bushes lay on the ground, stripped of their leaves, their branches like broken fingers pointing nowhere. The river struggled to flow around mud-banks and scattered debris. Crouched in the roots of an overturned tree, I saw a red howler monkey. Da had told me how few of them were left, after animal smugglers dragged them from their homes to sell on the black market for exotic animals. Now, this monkey stared accusingly at me over its orange-red beard, like a fed-up old man, before disappearing into what remained of the swamp.

From Da, I knew that the swamp was home to so many plants and animals. Not only that, but it protected the land from hurricanes and storms. These wetlands kept the shore from washing away, and reclaimed land from the ever-hungry sea. I thought of all the mangrove trees that had been cleared for plantations, factories, highways, or housing settlements. Now, even more of it was gone. I wondered how long this place would take to recover.

As Adri and I walked on the edge of the river, the sun was high in the sky. It beat down on our faces, but we didn't stop to rest. I knew that if I sat down, I wouldn't be able to get back up. Adri seemed to have the same idea, because he kept moving quickly, not even looking back to see how I was doing.

After a long time, I could hear the piping of birds. Fiddler crabs crept carefully from their holes, rolling out balls of mud. They waved their claws as if to say goodbye and good riddance.

We walked until the river flowed through more sand than mud, and the air had the sharp salty smell of the sea. Ahead of us, a rough bank of white rock blocked our view. The river cut through it. Without a word, we took off our shoes and waded through the shallow water between the high, white, pitted walls.

We came out on a long beach, lined with yellow sand stretching to a forested peninsula. Behind us, the sand was backed by a wall of white rock that was filled with caves and holes of various sizes.

Adri stared out at the sea. It was turquoise in the shallows and darker green as it went out, lined with white cresting waves.

"We finally made it," I whispered.

"Yeah," Adri muttered.

He didn't seem too relieved. We were one step closer to home, but still a long way from any kind of safety.

A pelican skimmed the waves then dived in. It came up with a beating fish. On the sand to my left, where the mouth of the river met the sea, a gang of egrets fought over a crab. The crab fought back, snapping at their beaks with its large claw.

I thought about how the sea had brought us all to

this island, in so many different ways. I prayed that, as Adri and I followed the water's edge, it would help us find our way back home.

Wait. Home. I looked at Cap'n Peg's sleeping face, hanging upside down from the branch in Adri's hands. The web portal! How could I have been so stupid? Once she woke up, Cap'n Peg could make a web portal that would get us home right away!

My heart rose like a kite on Easter Sunday. New strength poured into my tired legs.

"Adri, you genius! Cap'n Peg can take us home!"

"You just got that?" Adri snapped, checking to see if she was awake.

She wasn't, but I was so relieved I couldn't stop talking. "She can get us back to the village, my parents!"

I faltered. I could see Adri's face clearly now. It was twisted with fear and worry.

"We can get help to go back for your parents," I mumbled.

I didn't say, 'If they're still alive.'

I didn't want to think about what I hadn't told him, what I'd learned in his lost memories. In that last memory, I could still see his parents being dragged under the waves, fighting whatever had them in its grip, shouting for their only son to get to safety.

My heart beat hard in my chest. I thought about my parents, their love, the lessons they'd taught me even after the divorce – the person they were raising me to be. Not a liar or a coward, but someone with courage.

After everything we'd been through, Adri deserved to know the truth. I looked down at my grimy shoes.

"Adri, I have something to tell you..."

He turned to look at me, with a line forming between his eyebrows that made him look even more like his mother.

"Let me go, you lily-livered clod-stompers!"

Adri jumped. I nearly fell over.

"Cut me loose before I slice you from bow to stern!" Cap'n Peg was awake and fighting against the vine that Adri had used to tie her up.

"Great! You're awake," I pleaded, "please send us home!"

Adri held on to the branch tightly, while she spit and squirmed.

"Where's my crew? What did you do to them!" Her red robotic eye spun around wildly.

"Stop it," Adri ordered, giving the branch a little shake, "they're back at what's left of the dome. Don't you remember?"

It seemed like she did.

Cap'n Peg's whole body stiffened, and her one eye burned, "You two-legged fools... I have to go back now!"

"We are not going back to the swamp," I said firmly, "take us home."

"Not the swamp, you scurvy curs!" Cap'n shook her head, still twisting and trying to get free. "The Zoo..." she muttered, "while it's still there."

Adri froze.

"What do you mean?" I stuttered.

Cap'n Peg rolled her one good eye. "What I mean is they're leaving. The Council. The lab. Once a test goes this far wrong, that's it."

She counted: "Overeager X, Yara gone rogue, that beast blowing up half the swamp... It'll attract too much attention. It's burn and exit time."

"We got," she looked at an imaginary watch on her metal leg, "maybe an hour. Tops."

My face went numb.

"Burn?" I heard Adri repeat blankly.

"Did I stutter?" Cap'n Peg asked irritably. "The

Council will ship out everyone and everything at the research centre, and burn the rest. Whatever's left in the swamp, in the X's holes, the Zoo – everything and anything that can be tied back to them – pouf!" Cap'n Peg's telescope eye snapped out and then back in. "Up in smoke."

I stared at her, stunned. So that was how the Council planned to cover their tracks: a giant forest fire! I was horrified just thinking about the damage that could cause and how far it could spread.

Then the worst part dawned on me, just as Adri said it out loud.

"My parents!" he gasped hoarsely.

"What parents?" Cap'n Peg asked carelessly, trying to twist herself free.

"Don't act like you don't know!" Adri shook the branch hard. "My parents. If they're trapped at the Zoo, they'll be killed! Or taken who knows where. I'll never see them again!" His eyes were wild as he shouted.

"Hey!" Cap'n Peg growled. "Watch it Tarzan. You only this tough when I'm tied up! I don't know who you're talking about. The Zoo's a big place. I don't see everyone who comes in and out."

I couldn't tell if she was lying or telling the truth.

"Adri, stop it, please," I begged him, trying to stop him from smashing the branch and Cap'n Peg to pieces. "How do we even know they're there?"

"Stop that, you weak-hearted mollusc!" Cap'n Peg ordered shakily, after she stopped bouncing and swaying, looking like she was about to throw up.

"Okay," I rushed in when I saw the look on Adri's face, "we can go through a web portal to the village, get help, then take them through another portal back to the Zoo to look for your parents!"

"Nope," Cap'n Peg announced flatly. "Cut me loose and I can open up a portal to the village. But I not hanging around waiting for you to come back with your daddy, tantie, uncle and cousins, with guns and pitchforks and who knows what else."

"Can you say something helpful?" I pointed out.

She rolled her eyes at me like, Nah.

Adri muttered, "Truth is, they probably wouldn't even believe us. Or they'd be so freaked out by a talking spider and magic web that by the time we got everyone on board, my parents would be long gone."

"Facts," Cap'n Peg sucked her teeth. "You never know what a Two-Legs will do." She waved a leg scornfully. "Besides, I can't expose Anansi magic to the villagers. The Council would have my neck for that. You two have seen way too much already. You lucky to still be alive."

My blood ran cold. Lucky wasn't how I'd describe it. Adri was staring off into the distance like we weren't even there. He looked like a guitar string about to snap.

"How do we know you won't just run off when we let you go," I pressed, trying to keep the panic from my voice, "without even making the portal?"

"You don't!" Cap'n Peg cackled.

"Enough!" Adri's voice cut through the air. "I'm going to get my parents. Now."

He looked at me with red-rimmed eyes that said: 'You coming or not?'

Cap'n Peg coughed loudly and deliberately.

"Hey girlie," she pointed at me with her metallic claw, "just say the word and you'll be back in Samaan Bay in no time. I can take this rock-headed boy to the Zoo by himself. You don't need to follow his madness."

"Yeah, you should go," Adri said softly, turning away.

I thought of Mum and Da, worrying and wondering where I was. Knowing Jake, he was probably out looking for me too. He'd only ever been kind to me, trying to find things that I'd enjoy doing, to include me in the new version of our family. I'd even be happy to see the Terror right now. I was so close to being with them again, I could taste it.

Then I remembered Kala and Yara fighting for each other, even to the very end. Was I worse than the person I'd called a monster?

"Hey! We don't have all day!" Cap'n Peg interrupted, poking at Adri with one of her hairy legs. "Burn and exit, remember? We gotta up anchor now!" Her voice deepened and shook like the air before a storm. "Remember, dead men tell no tales."

How had this spider become a pirate? I guessed that was a story for another day.

"I'm coming with you," I sighed.

Adri stared at me, his eyes warm and damp. "You sure?"

"I'm sure," I murmured, "but first..."

If we were going to risk our lives, he should make that choice knowing the truth.

"I have something to tell you," I spit out.

Between Cap'n Peg's rude interruptions, I told Adri about my visions. I told him everything that I'd felt and seen about his parents and what they'd done to protect him in the end.

Adri was silent. The wind whipped around us. My heart flopped like a fish out of water. A cloud of darkness took over his face.

Before I could say anything else, he grabbed the branch with Cap'n Peg tied to it and stormed off.

"Crazy two-legs," she screeched, "we don't have time for this!"

"Adri!" I shouted, running after him. "I didn't know how to tell you. Or if you'd believe me..."

"You!" He turned on me with a fury that I'd never seen before.

His eyes looked black; the pupils so wide that they were like an eclipse.

"You think that everything is about you," his voice broke. "I don't care what you saw, or what you think you saw. My parents are still alive!"

"Okay, then I'm coming with you!" I begged, but I could see from his face that it was already too late.

"Stop!" He shouted over the sound of the surf. "All this time... You knew what had happened, you saw my memories, and you didn't even try to tell me?" His voice rose higher with each word.

He backed away from me with every step that I took toward him.

"Listen girlie," Cap'n Peg argued from her vine

and branch prison, "let this mad boy go. You don't need a portal. Go north along the sea here, and in no time, you'll find a village. From there, they can take you to Samaan Bay."

I ignored her.

"Adri," I begged, "let me explain."

His eyes were empty, cold. "I think you've done more than enough."

He grabbed Cap'n Peg and ran down the beach to our right, heading for a spot where tall grey rocks made a kind of barrier across the sand. I didn't know what he'd say if I followed him.

"Hey, watch it boy!" Cap'n Peg protested. "I am not a ball. Stop bouncing me around." Then she shouted back at me: "Remember: go north. Follow the coast!"

Why was she so keen to get rid of me? I heard her instructions but kept looking at Adri. He had paused and was staring out at the waves with a mixture of hatred, longing and fear.

"I'm so sorry," I said over and over.

Only the salt breeze answered me.

Adri balanced on top of the sharp rocks.

"Thanks a lot!"

I wasn't sure if he meant that for his parents or me.

Then he jumped down to the other side of the rocks and disappeared.

Chapter Nineteen
SHOCK

I sat in the sand alone, watching the surf try to grab my shoes.

Shh, shh. It hushed me, like a mother comforting a child, or a friend whispering a warning.

There was a tiny shell next to my left hand. The delicate swirls made me think of Baby Tayo's ears. I pictured his round, dimpled, fat-cheeked face.

I'd messed everything up, at home and here too.

My stomach hurt.

"This one's for you T," I whispered, tossing the shell back into the sea.

The wind blew spitty kisses into my face and hair, as if to say, 'You too sis.'

I sat there limply until, suddenly, I heard a faint sound. I spun around then exhaled sharply in relief. Behind me on the beach, a group of baby leatherback turtles was hatching. They had broken out of their slightly gel-like round eggs and were crawling up out of the nest their mother had so carefully hidden in the sand.

I had come to the northeast coast with my dad to see these giant turtles lay eggs at night, hauling their bodies out of the roaring surf like prehistoric dinosaurs and sending sand flying as they dug their nests with back flippers as big as oars. These babies' mother was miles away by now, swimming in some far sea. For now, they only had each other.

With a rustle of wings, two dark corbeaux with wrinkled grey heads and necks landed near the nest. I jumped up and shooed them away. Of the hundreds of eggs laid, few baby turtles would even make it the short distance to the sea. I stood guard over them as they flopped over the sand, sometimes flipping over, trying to get used to their four tiny flat flippers. Their little grey-black bodies had white, long, thin ridges on their shells, just like the mother they might never see. But each baby could fit in the palm of my hand, while mother leatherbacks, the largest of all sea-turtles, were able to grow up to seven feet long, 2000 pounds, and live up to a hundred years or more.

These babies, like their mother, once they survived and grew, through some inner compass, would come back to lay their eggs on this same beach where they were born. In the meantime, they would go on epic journeys across the oceans of the world, visiting so many places that I longed to see.

I watched how the baby turtles kept hopping and scooting towards the water, despite the burning sand, blistering sun, and all the threats waiting for them above and below. When they hit the water, their awkward movements turned to music. Like ballerinas dancing or kites in the air, they took to the sea.

"Swim well," I whispered, as the last baby turtle crested the surf and was gone.

I looked down at their tracks in the sand. If they hadn't given up, neither would I.

Adri was probably long gone by now, through the web portal with Cap'n Peg, searching the Zoo for his parents. If the Council was as dangerous as it seemed, he would need all the help he could get.

The first step was to find someone, anyone with a phone. I dashed the tears from my eyes. Cap'n Peg had said to go north along the coast, and I'd find a village. There was no more time to mope. I had work to do.

"Zo."

I spun around in shock. Adri was standing behind me, his hands empty, his face strained.

"You came back," my voice caught in my throat.

"Yeah," he mumbled.

"Where's Cap'n Peg?" I asked, trying not to let him see me cry.

Adri grimaced. "She's heavy... I put her in a cave on the other side of those rocks." He pointed with his chin. "Let's get some water and get back over there. We don't have much time."

I tried to meet his eyes. "I'm so sorry."

"Okay," he avoided looking at me, "you thirsty?"

I could tell that he was trying to keep calm.

"Yes," I answered, happy to just have another chance.

We walked over to the shallow stream on my left. It bubbled over smooth stones to the sea. I bent over to drink and wash my tear-stained face. I felt a quick movement behind me and turned to see Adri with a stone lifted high in both hands, swinging it down toward my head.

There was no time to think. I flung myself backwards out of the way of the stone, ending up on my back in the small stream. In a flash, Adri was on me, his long hands around my throat. I pulled my chin down to my chest, trying to break his hold. I shoved his shoulders, banged on his arms and back as hard as I could, but he didn't even flinch.

Rage filled Adri's face.

"You fool!" He smiled viciously.

My fingers clawed at his eyes. He didn't budge.

"Your good friend Adri," he sang in a mocking voice. "Little girl, you have no idea..." His face was twisted with fury.

I kept fighting. It was like being in a nightmare without being able to wake up. I fought to breathe.

He shrieked, "I escaped once, but she didn't. I had to go back... They caught me again, experimented on us both."

Who was he talking about? I felt like I was going mad. My body grew weak as I ran out of air. Adri's face blurred. I closed my eyes, let myself go limp. Maybe if he thought I'd passed out, I would have a chance. His hands stayed around my throat, but he moved off my shins.

"Don't worry," he chuckled evilly. "However long it takes, I will find out exactly what you know."

Without moving, I focused on the muscles of my legs, getting ready to knee Adri hard and give myself a chance to break free.

****

Instead, I opened my eyes in a thick forest. I was standing, staring into the face of an old woman in a dress and head-tie of coarse brown-cotton. I was back in a vision, while Adri attacked me. I hoped I survived to come out of it.

The woman in front of me was tall with such rich black skin that she looked indigo in the shade under the trees. She had the stunning, perfectly carved features of a Benin statue, but with a raised scar that ran all the way down her right cheek, from eyes like deep pools. I wondered what had caused the scar, but the person whose memory I was in seemed to feel a wave of love and familiarity for this woman, laced with a nameless fear.

Something moved softly against my leg. I looked down quickly to see that I was dressed in a worn cotton shirt and pants. A large hound, almost as tall as my waist, stood close, looking up at me with knowing amber eyes. I put one hand on its warm, fuzzy head. My heart skipped a beat. I should be in one of Adri's memories, but the hand petting this dog didn't belong to him. It was small, dark brown, delicate. What was happening? This wasn't Adri's body I was trapped in. It wasn't his mind. None of this made any sense. How did Adri have someone else's memory? I felt anxiety bubble up inside me, but couldn't tell whether it was coming from me, or from the person whose mind I was in.

"Try again now," the old woman told me, taking my chin gently in one calloused hand.

Try what? I had no idea. The woman wasn't speaking English, yet I understood every word as if it were my mother tongue. What was it? French? No, some form of Creole. We were somewhere in the heart of a tropical forest, not so different from the one around Rain-Tree Hill. The air felt moist and warm. Everything around me was lush and green and alive.

"I can't Maman," I murmured in a singsong voice that wasn't mine. With shock, I realized that it was a girl's voice – a voice that seemed vaguely familiar.

"I'm not like Kala," I found myself saying, "she can do anything."

Kala! Why was Kala in this memory and what did this moment have to do with Adri? I tried to turn my head to look for Kala but, just like in the other visions, I was not in control of this body. Instead, I found myself looking down at the glossy hound, its mouth lolling open in a smile.

My mind tumbled and took a while to right itself when the dog said, "Not anything, just animals."

The dog had spoken with the raspy voice of another girl. Before my eyes, the large dog changed into a blue-chested peacock, its tail fanning out into bright colours. The peacock dwindled to an anxious white rabbit with a snuffling pink nose. Then, in the blink of an eye, the rabbit was a Monarch butterfly with orange and black wings like stained-glass, hanging in the air. My mind whirled. Kala was the Flesh-skinner – at least when I'd met her. Now I could tell that she was a lagahoo, a creature Da had told me about in stories: a shapeshifter.

Yet, the person whose memory I was in felt no surprise at all.

"Show off," was all she tossed out, rolling her eyes, as I sat invisibly inside her mind, wondering what on earth was going on.

Suddenly, the butterfly next to me became a short, curvy, freckled girl with a wide grin, her reddish hair in a wiry afro pulled back from her face with a bright band of blue cloth. It was Yara's sister, Kala!

I thought of the last time I'd seen her as the Flesh-skinner, lying on the ground in the middle of the ruined dome, surrounded by broken X. Yet here she was, years earlier it seemed, in this memory - a girl with the amazing ability to change into the shape of any animal she wanted.

"Don't be jealous 'cause I'm not scared like you!" Kala said saucily to the person whose memory I was in, pursing her lips, her head cocked to one side.

Now I could guess whose memory this was, but how was it possible?

"Girls!" The woman I'd called Maman grabbed my attention. Her face was creased with worry, puckering the scar on her cheek. "We don't have much time."

I felt the terror mixed with loyalty and bravery, running between me and these women, connecting the three of us like an electrical current.

The girl called Kala was solemn now.

"Sorry Maman."

She turned her light-filled amber eyes to me. "You have to try. Without you, we'll be caught before we make it to the Free Village."

The old woman, Maman, was looking at me too, as if they were both waiting on me to do something.

"Okay," I felt my lips saying. "Okay."

A peculiar sensation came over me: a tingling, fiery feeling. I breathed hoarsely, my chest heaving, like I was lifting a great weight. I stared down at the hands and arms I had just started getting used to. They grew larger and longer, changing from thin and dark, to pale and muscular, covered with fine blond hairs. I felt a wave of nausea. What was happening? I could feel the bones and muscles move inside my body, my face. I was changing to look like someone else.

****

I came out of the memory just in time to see the shock on Adri's face as he slid off to one side, out cold. I hacked and coughed, trying to catch my breath and make sense of what I was seeing. Somehow, a second Adri was looking down at me with a large wet stone in his hands. He'd used it to knock the first Adri out. He put down the stone and tried to pull me to my feet.

Two Adris! That was too many. I hit and kicked at him weakly. My eyes swung from his grim, bruised face, to the face of the person lying next to me. They were both the same - like identical twins - one, lying there and the other standing in front of me, looking as horrified as I felt.

Then the unconscious Adri's face and body began to melt and change. Instead of a second Adri, I found myself staring down at Yara, stretched out motionless in the sand next to the stream.

Chapter Twenty
SPEED

"Come on!" Adri shouted, forcing me to run.

My mind was in a haze. It went from Adri to Yara and back again, trying to process what I'd just seen. Adri had tried to kill me. No, not Adri. Yara had made herself look like him.

I'd fallen into one of Yara's memories: seen her mother and Kala when she was a little girl. So, Yara was a shapeshifter too, like her sister. But whereas Kala had changed into animals before she was the Flesh-skinner, Yara could make herself look like other people.

She had mimicked Adri – looked and sounded just like him. I felt cold. Creatures like this had terrified me, even in stories. Now, I was finding out that they were real.

Speaking of creatures... "Adri, where's Cap'n Peg?" Had Yara done something to her?

"Gone. No time. To look." Adri panted, never slowing down.

We sped along the beach to the forested peninsula. It seemed like miles away. I realized that he was trying to get us to the trees, where we could find somewhere to hide before Yara woke up. But, running on shifting sand wasn't easy. We had covered half the distance when I looked back and saw Yara getting slowly to her feet.

"Adri!" I warned him, my voice cracking.

He glanced back and without a word, picked up speed. When I looked back over my shoulder, Yara was gone and in her place was a man with the broad chest and powerful legs of a world-famous sprinter. He raced towards us with huge strides, kicking up jets of sand in his wake. Adri took one look at the man cutting down the distance between us, then at the still-distant line of trees.

"Come on, this way!" He pushed me, climbing over the tall wall of grey rocks that cut across the sand. We ducked down behind them, out of Yara's view, and scrambled towards the white line of cliffs at the back of the beach.

Where was he taking us?

"In!"

He pointed to one of many holes at the base of the craggy, uneven cliff.

I stood there, staring at it blankly. Did he expect me to go in there? He looked behind us frantically, then bent down and squeezed through the low entry. I came to my senses as his feet disappeared. I bent all the way down and scrambled into the hole, almost knocking my head against the jagged rock walls. The tunnel was just a little wider than my body, with a roof so low that I could only crawl on my stomach, pulling myself along the sandy floor in darkness. Ahead of me, I could hear Adri's scuffling feet. I wondered what would happen if the tunnel got too small for us to pass through. Would we stay in here trapped like fossils, or have to wriggle backwards the entire way, to face a vengeful Yara at the end?

I felt like I was suffocating in the narrow space. Worst of all, I thought that I could hear, some distance behind me, muffled breathing, and the scrabbling sound of someone coming after us. Any second, I expected to feel Yara's burning hands grab my feet. My chest tightened to the point where I could hardly breathe.

Just when I thought that the tunnel would never end, I saw a faint glimmer of light and the soles of Adri's shoes, dropping out of sight. I scrambled after him and fell forwards with a splash. I saw my hands on the ground in front of me, my fingers splayed in a shallow pool of water.

I got to my feet slowly. Adri was spinning around like a trapped animal, looking for another way out. I moved away from the hole behind me and looked around. We were in a cylindrical cave, about four times as wide as the span of my arms. The sandy floor was covered with shallow saltwater puddles. The craggy walls were steep and wet. Sunlight filtered down from a small porthole in the rock ceiling high above us. Even if we could climb the walls, we wouldn't fit through that space. There was nowhere to go.

I could hear movement in the tunnel we'd just escaped. Adri's face was wet and covered with grit. He narrowed his eyes. He looked more angry than afraid. I was just tired of running.

At his signal, I pressed myself silently to one side of the hole leading in and out of the tunnel. He stood on the other side. The noise in the tunnel was getting closer. Adri bent down and slid the knife from Yara's house out of his shoe. I tried not to breathe too loudly.

A pair of hands reached out of the tunnel. They were small, flushed pink and shockingly cute. The hands grasped the bottom edge of the hole and pulled. Out, face downwards, popped a head of long golden hair.

Adri pounced, grabbed the tiny arms, and pulled a little blond girl, not more than seven years old, out of the tunnel. She was dressed in a polka-dot jersey and pants, covered head to toe with sand and dirt. She smiled as Adri held her arms behind her back. Her wide green eyes sparkled. I searched her face, but there was no trace of Yara there.

"Don't move," Adri warned her, tightening his grip on her arms.

"Or what?" the girl said in a high sweet voice. "You wouldn't hurt a child, now would you?" She laughed a tinkling doll's laugh.

"Enough!" Adri snapped. "Don't try to get in our heads. It won't work."

"Not your head," the girl said quietly, staring at me, "hers."

I stared into the little girl's sparkling eyes. They were blue-green like the sea.

"I finally figured it out," the girl continued in a whisper. "Do you want to know the truth Zo?"

"Enough," Adri's voice was strained, like he was about to snap.

"Don't," I begged.

I wasn't sure if I was pleading with Yara or Adri.

The little girl's starry laugh echoed through the cavern. Suddenly, she slammed her head back into Adri's chest and spun out of his grip. Adri staggered back. With uncanny strength, she kicked me toward the rock wall, before turning on Adri.

I struggled painfully to my feet.

"Stay back!" Adri shouted, as the girl, morphing into Yara with each step, closed in on him.

He faced Yara awkwardly, waving the knife from her kitchen in front of him like a flag.

"Or what?" Yara hissed, moving in.

Suddenly, Adri's body language changed.

He was taller, stronger, more balanced somehow, confident and in control. My mind spun and kept spinning. They began to fight, lightning-fast, using martial arts that were quicker and more intricate than any I had ever seen. I staggered back against the wall, as they parried each other's blows. Yara leapt, spun, and dove in the tight space to evade

Adri's strikes. He did the same thing; jumping over her sweeping kicks and flipping backwards off the rock walls to avoid her punches. I ducked and stumbled from side to side, trying to stay out of their way.

I couldn't believe my eyes. When had Adri learned to fight like this and why hadn't he done this in the battle with the X? Something was deeply wrong. Part of me wanted to inch toward the tunnel and crawl away, but I hesitated. After everything Adri and I had been through, I couldn't just leave him here. I'd waited so long to tell him about falling into his memories and what had happened to his parents. So what if he hadn't told me that he was a ninja? We had both kept secrets from each other.

But, what else hadn't he told me and why?

Yara ran up the side of the cavern and jumped over Adri, turning in the air and knocking the knife from his hand. It went skidding across the floor. She closed in on him, but Adri blocked her blows with his arms, then spun around her at the speed of light, grabbing her neck in a tight hold.

"Zo, the knife!" he shouted.

I picked it up slowly and backed away to the far wall of the cavern.

"How come...?" I stammered. "Why didn't you...?"

Yara struggled against his grip. She spat and laughed.

"Zo, give me the knife!" Adri ordered. "Let's end this."

What did he mean, 'end' it? Images of everything we had been through together flashed across my mind. I saw Adri from the time I'd dragged him from the river to the moment he had swung his net into mine and cut me free. I thought of the visions, when I had been part of his memories for a few moments, seeing the faces of his parents, feeling his love and pain and fear and joy as if they were my own.

My shoulders slumped under a huge weight.

"I can't," I whispered.

"What?" Adri hissed furiously.

The boy I'd known would never hurt someone, at least that's what I'd thought. And I had lived in Yara's memory too, felt her loss and love for her family.

Yara was staring at me, surprised, with the smile wiped from her cheeks. Her face softened briefly. We all froze for a moment, suspended in time. Then Yara ripped free of Adri's grasp and flung him back against the wall behind her. She charged at me so quickly that I only had time to step back, the knife still clutched in my right hand.

I felt something wet trickle down my shirt. I was sitting on the floor of the cavern. Yara knelt in front of me, her eyes glistening. I stared back at her in concern. Was she hurt? I coughed and felt a stab of pain. When I looked down, I saw the knife. Yara had struggled with me, and it had stuck me by accident. I felt light-headed.

Adri pushed Yara away. My head slid gently back to the hard ground. My shirt was wet and cold. I could hear my heart thump loudly in my ears. I gasped as Adri pressed down on the wound with the edge of my shirt, careful not to touch my skin.

"Get us out of here now!" he shouted.

How did he expect Yara to rescue us? Even if she got us out of the cave, where would we find help in the middle of nowhere? Waves of nausea washed over me. My stomach hurt.

My ears rang like they were full of water. I opened my eyes to see Adri yelling down at me in the white-walled cave. I was lying face-up on the ground. A searing pain burned my stomach. Yara was nowhere to be seen.

"Zo, hold on!" I could see Adri shout down at me, but I could barely hear his voice.

It was like looking up at him from underwater.

Then I saw it. Behind Adri, a giant spiderweb was growing in a beautiful, intricate design. I could hear drums. The spiderweb became clear like a mirror and out of it jumped Cap'n Peg and her crew.

Somehow, it was great to see them.

"Come on girlie," she said gently, "time to go."

Her metal arm whirred quietly, lifting my head.

A spider wearing cut-off jeans on all of its scrawny legs whispered loudly, "Wait nah. After all that... she gone and dead?"

The other spiders steupsed and snorted in disgust. Cap'n Peg shut them up with one cutting look.

"Breathe girlie," she ordered, "breathe."

I tried to laugh, but my lips wouldn't move. Adri, the cave, Cap'n Peg, and everything around me faded. I was floating up in the air. I looked back at the shrinking world. The faces of my family rushed past me like stars, flashing in the darkness. I didn't have time to say goodbye. I hoped they knew how much I loved them.

Up ahead, there was a white spot of light that

grew as I flew toward it. I wanted to say, "I'm not ready," but it was too late.

I thought about everything I'd heard about life after death. I wished I'd thought about it more before.

Chapter Twenty-One
SPLINTER

I woke up suspended in what felt like water. Was this the afterlife, or was I stuck in another person's memory? This body seemed like mine, but I couldn't be sure. I opened my eyes and found myself blinded by a bright white light. I blinked until my eyes cleared. I was floating upright in electric-blue liquid, like a cloudless patch of island sky. Somehow, I could still breathe. There was a kind of oxygen mask on my face. My hands fumbled over it. Better not to take it off until I got out of... this.

I tried to move, but something kept me in place. My fingers touched a cold invisible barrier. Gradually, the things around me took form. I was in a glass cylinder in an all-white windowless room. The blue of the liquid around me was the only colour, and the room was bare except for me. The spiders were gone. So were Adri and Yara. My heart thumped inside my chest. I could hear myself breathe. The faint taste of salt on my tongue comforted me. It reminded me of the sea.

I looked down. My heart beat wildly in my ears. It was my body alright, stuck in this glass can. There were thin white tubes running from the veins in my arms. They ran around behind me. I couldn't turn my head far enough to see what they were attached to. Suddenly, I remembered the knife. I felt for the wound in the middle of my stomach. There was nothing but a small, raised scar just above my navel. It didn't even hurt. I was healed... How long had I been in here?

I used my hands to check for more tubes. As far as I could tell, my chest was wrapped in a soft white cloth and my hips were fully encased in what felt like hard plastic, with larger tubes coming from it as well.

"Centre alert! Centre alert!" A robotic voice blared suddenly, as if over a loudspeaker.

I jumped, looking around as far as I could. The room was still empty, except for me.

"Self-destruct in 15 minutes!" the speaker warned.

"All personnel prepare for transport."

Centre alert? Self-destruct. Transport?

My heart thumped in my ears. Of course. I was at the Zoo.

The same Zoo that, according to Cap'n Peg, would be going up in flames, as the Council made their exit and covered their tracks. Fifteen minutes. That was it? I had to get out of here. I kicked the glass and struggled against whatever held me in place, but I couldn't break free.

I tried to feel for a lever within the cylinder, a hinge or button of some kind that I could use to get out. My fingers felt nothing but liquid and glass. I hit the glass with my hands. It didn't even shake.

Just then, a door opened in the white wall to my left and Adri walked in.

Relief flooded my body. I banged on the glass silently. Adri was dressed in a spotless white tunic, with soft white shoes. He didn't look at me or acknowledge me in any way. I grew still, anxiety creeping up my neck. Why wasn't he helping me get out of here?

Instead, he walked directly to the middle of the room and a white console grew up from the floor. There was no other way to describe it. It was as though the room was made of some movable, living material. It grew him a smooth white chair. Adri sat and put his hands on the console. A red light scanned him from head to toe and images began to flash above his head. There were photos and videos of our time together – me rescuing him from drowning, us under attack from the Flesh-skinner, him being kidnapped by the X, the battle with Yara and Kala, everything.

A picture of me popped up over his head. Around it, were images that looked like medical results: CT scans, MRI readouts, X-rays. There were graphs and streaming data. How had he collected all this information without me knowing? I banged soundlessly on the glass of my cage.

Adri turned to look at me and I stopped cold. His eyes weren't his. They were bright red, like the light on an X's forehead.

"De-activate Cryotube A," Adri said in a calm, oddly computer-like voice.

The blue liquid around me seeped down into some invisible drainage system. The tubes slid painlessly from my body and the oxygen mask opened and lifted away. Soft cloth came down over my body as the tubes disappeared. I was left standing in the empty cylinder in a seamless, knee-length white tunic like Adri's. White, sandal-like shoes came up from a hidden compartment and encased my feet. The glass silently opened. I paused, then stepped out into the room. Anything was better than that prison. Around me, everything was as white and smooth as porcelain. The room was cold, but the shoes on my feet were surprisingly warm.

"Adri, what's going on?" I asked, making my voice sound bolder than I felt.

I stared at his shining red eyes. What had they done to him?

"Come, come, we don't have much time," Adri said in that smooth, mechanical voice, with a thin, irritated smile.

"Why are you talking like that?" I asked, my voice rising.

"I am Symbiotic Test Subject 1," the voice said, with that terrifying imitation of a smile, "you can call me SYM now instead of Adri. It is more accurate."

Symbiosis? From Biology class, I knew that this was when two creatures lived in a close relationship, with at least one of them being dependent on the other.

I took a step back. "Symbiotic...with what?"

"The boy Adri and the computer that runs this lab, of course," the SYM said with a heavy serving of scorn. "Take a look."

A screen appeared above the console. It was playing a video. In it, I could see Adri on a metal bed of some kind. His eyes were closed; his chest rose and fell like he was asleep. Suddenly, a metal needle snapped into place above his head, with what looked like a computer chip on its point. It lowered toward Adri's head. I felt sick but couldn't look away. Just as it was about to reach him, the screen disappeared.

"No need for the gory details," Adri said, smiling widely, "all you need to know is that the chip in my brain connects me to the Council's computer system, and I to it. Together, we're called SYM.

"Chip? Lab?" I repeated numbly.

My brain spun. So, Adri had been working for the Council all this time! No. Not Adri. Whatever they'd turned him into.

I stared around me in a daze. I was trapped by the Council that the spiders had warned me about; the Council that Yara had worked for and hated. They'd been watching me all this time.

"Our insect drones tranquilized you on Rain-Tree Hill," Adri went on in that superior tone, as if he knew what I was thinking. "Our Watcher is very thorough. She's been watching you pack your little runaway bag for some days now."

My mind was a jumble of words. "Watcher? ... My bag... You mean Ms. K?"

Adri nodded with a grim smile.

"Too bad," he said thoughtfully, "she must be dealt with severely for the warnings she gave you. Watchers are a bit of an... untamed element. But she will have to learn to play by the rules. I have already reported her to the Council," his lips curled scornfully, "along with every one of her eight-legged helpers."

"The spiders!" I burst out.

"Of course. The Watchers, the gnat-drones, the X, Kala, Yara, they all work, or shall we say worked, for us. Unfortunately, there were... complications. This is the first time that field-tests have been allowed on such a wide scale. The contained environment of our labs is much easier to manage," he droned on.

Anger bubbled up in my chest. Betrayal, lies, tests!

"Why were you testing me?"

The SYM scoffed, distorting Adri's usually kind face. "Testing you! No, not you child. Me! This is the first time a SYM has been ready for testing in the field," it said proudly, puffing out Adri's narrow chest. "We needed to see if we could convince you, a gifted child, to trust us. You know what they say, nothing ventured, nothing gained!"

I was speechless.

"We needed someone like you – new to your gift – to test the SYM, to see if you would eventually confide in it, tell it all about your gift and what you could do. You did, by the beach. So-o-o touching!" The SYM laughed, making Adri's face look cruel. "Now we can use the SYM to get close to other gifted children. To get them to show Adri, and us, what they can really do – to gain their trust and have them show him the full extent of their abilities."

Other gifted children? So, there were others like me. And the Council was going to use Adri, with that chip in his brain, to trick them into trusting him, to betray them to the Council. Anger brought hot tears to my eyes, but I blinked them back. I refused to let them see me cry.

"We are masters of cover. See for yourself," the SYM offered, clapping its hands twice.

All the walls around us faded, including the ceiling and floor. I screamed, looking for something to hold on to, then realized that I was standing on glass or some other transparent material. Around me was nothing but bright day sky. I looked down just in time to see the long, squirming legs of the ship turn transparent, and disappear. The whole vessel was shaped like a jellyfish. I'd never seen anything like it. Tremors ran up and down my arms.

"Are you guys aliens?" I stammered, backing away.

That thing that looked like Adri laughed, then answered in the SYM's fake, smooth voice. "No. This is simply a mobile lab made for the Council's, shall we say, private research. Think of it as a few years ahead of most planes," it added with a mocking smile.

I guess I was glad they were human, but the rest of that explanation wasn't comforting. I looked down again slowly.

We were hovering over a small hill in the mountains that looked like an old, eroded volcano, its sides covered with grass and trees, with a crater on top. In the crater, was a circular compound dotted with grey concrete buildings. The spaces in-between were lined with X, moving in orderly, army-like rows.

At the heart of the compound was a single building shaped like a white, vertical rectangle, surrounded by a concrete circular yard. Everything was ringed by the Zoo's towering wall. From up here, I could see that beyond the wall was the forest, but within the circle, the building and its surrounding compound didn't have one single tree.

I felt dizzy. The Zoo. The place I'd most wanted to avoid, haunted by the creatures we'd barely escaped in the forest, and who knows what else. When had this vessel taken off from there? Our exit had been so smooth, I hadn't even noticed. But it made sense that I wasn't hearing the 'Centre self-destruct' alerts anymore.

"W-wha...? How?" I had so many questions.

What had happened to the Zoo's old, broken-down buildings? Anyone who flew over this site could see that it was far from abandoned.

"Watch this," the fake Adri boasted, putting some codes into the console.

My breath caught in my throat. As it typed in the codes, the Zoo changed before my eyes; from a neat compound full of perfectly shaped buildings, to a collection of broken-down sheds, overgrown by forest.

Camouflage. Of course.

The SYM had called the vessel we were in a mobile lab. Well, if it was mobile, why weren't we moving further away, before the Zoo below us erupted into flames? We were just hanging there, at what I hoped was a safe distance above the compound, as if Adri... the SYM... was waiting for something.

Maybe it was supervising the self-destruct of the Zoo from here, making sure that all the evidence was removed. Someone or something else was probably monitoring the self-destruct sequences at the ruined dome in the swamp and the X's underground caves – making sure to clean up whatever was left of the rogue creatures in the forest. As I watched the X who were crawling in orderly lines between the buildings, I felt sorry for them. They were made, used and then destroyed: only built for whatever the Council wanted.

"Who else works here?" I wondered out loud.

It was one thing to hide this place, but how were they getting staff in and out unnoticed. Was it in more floating labs like this one?

"The entire facility is computer and AI operated, guarded by the X," the SYM said smugly, "with additional resources in the field, like Yara and Kala, the Watchers - or spiders, as you know them - and more X."

My stomach churned. I felt like throwing up. Everything Yara had said was true. She, Kala, and the X were the Council's competing servants.

What were they going to do with me?

I tried to gather my thoughts and glance around me for a way out, but the surfaces of the lab were still completely clear. It felt like I was standing in sky, surrounded by the high green mountains of the Northern Range. At another time, it might have been beautiful. Now, it was just terrifying.

The only solid thing that remained was the white chair and console at which the SYM sat. Yet I was sure that to the outside eye, looking up, there was no lab. It was well camouflaged too; invisible.

My skin was slimy with sweat. I panicked, fighting to catch my breath.

"Where are you going to take me?"

"Hold tight. You'll find out soon," the SYM smirked, twisting Adri's sweet, lopsided smile, "but of course, we have to wipe your memory first."

I looked at the red, soulless eyes of the boy I'd thought was my friend. "What?"

"That's why I woke you up of course," the SYM continued as if it were talking about a Sunday stroll, "can't do a memory-wipe through the liquid in the cryotubes."

"No..." I shook my head numbly.

A memory-wipe! Up to what point were they going to wipe my mind? Without my memories, I'd be defenceless, open to whatever lies the Council decided to feed me.

I backed away from the grinning SYM, choking on horror and rage.

"So, it was all fake, right Adri? The memories I saw in you – the boat, your parents, everything!"

"On the contrary," the SYM's slick voice responded from Adri's face, "we left the host Adri's memories, apart from his capture, intact. Given the reports from the Watcher, we knew your gift lay somewhere in the mind. It only made sense to leave Adri with most of his real memories, thoughts, and emotions for you to find."

My heart broke. I had fallen into Adri's memories, then hidden them from him, thinking that I was protecting him and keeping us focused on getting back to Samaan Bay alive. Meanwhile, the Council, had used his memories to lure me in, to test the SYM's abilities.

How was I any better than them? We both thought we knew what was best for others. We'd both tried to control Adri's choices. At the end of the day, Adri had deserved better than this, better than me.

"And your Mum's cancer," I cried, my voice breaking, "was that real too?"

At the mention of Adri's mum, the SYM's face contorted strangely, eyelids flickering wildly over the bright red eyes. Suddenly, the machine-like voice was gone, and Adri's hoarse voice broke out of his mouth, making me jump backwards in shock.

"Let me talk to her!" he begged.

He blinked hard and when his eyes opened, they were his own – dark brown and pleading. Adri shuddered, as if from an electric shock. He struggled to take a step toward me, fighting against an invisible force that was pulling him back. I flinched and ducked away, wondering if this was another trick.

"Please Zo! The Council's tech. It's in my head," Adri shook like a leaf, his eyes frantically searching mine, "I can't..."

The electric jolt ran through him again, stronger this time. Adri screamed. His eyes slammed shut. When he opened them, the red lights were back in place.

"As you can see," the SYM's voice had a slightly clipped tone. "The host subject Adri and I are deeply linked. He struggles at times to accept this."

My heart tried to break free from my chest. Adri was still here – part of his mind intact! The chip didn't have perfect control.

I took a small step toward him. "Adri, if you're in there, please fight this!"

The SYM sighed, speaking into the console, "Subjects are ready for memory-wipe and transfer. Raise Cryotube B please."

Just then, another glass cylinder rose up from the invisible floor. It was filled with green liquid. Yara floated inside, upright and unconscious, with white tubes coming from her nose and body. Trapped in the cylinder, she looked softer, less formidable. She was trapped too, just like me.

I had to find a way to get us out of here... Adri included.

The SYM's smile grew wider until Adri's face looked like it would split in two.

He turned to the console. "Memory-stick please."

I shrank back, but there was nowhere to go.

A viciously sharp, two-pronged silver rod emerged from the console. It looked like an oversized tuning fork. Adri waved it with one hand. The rod buzzed and zapped with a powerful surge of energy. He smiled with satisfaction and continued talking.

"Kala was an unfortunate loss. Her shape-changing ability was too strong for us to control at first, but, once we experimented on it over the years, she grew weaker, until she was stuck in that somewhat monstrous form. Even so, she had her uses."

Anger burned through my body. I wasn't going to let them use me the way they'd used everyone else.

The SYM stepped toward me, gripping the memory-stick in his hands. It flashed with energy that looked like small bursts of lightning.

"Adri," I shouted desperately, "wait! What about your parents?"

The SYM paused, then kept walking toward me.

"Your Ma and Dad. Shaving your heads. One year cancer-free, remember? Pity sucks!"

The SYM paused and shuddered. Its cold red eyes closed, then opened as Adri's deep brown eyes, crying, "Zo, help me!"

His eyes spun in his head, as the SYM fought to take over.

Grabbing my chance, I charged, knocking him to the ground, trying to wrestle the charged memory-stick from his hand. He looked up at me with Adri's warm eyes.

"Zo," he warned me, "watch out!"

I leapt away as he was hit from inside by another shock.

The SYM opened its red eyes and advised, "Stop. Resistance only brings more pain."

It pulled at me. I broke away, ran up to Yara's cylinder and beat frantically on the glass.

"Yara, wake up! Wake up!"

Adri groaned. His real eyes squinted with pain. Then they flipped back to glowing red dots.

The SYM grabbed me. I sank to the floor as it glared down at me. "Stop this at once...!"

It writhed and Adri's wide brown eyes stared at the memory-stick, that instrument of torture in his hand. He moved it toward me, then turned and slammed it into the console, zapping it with the memory-stick's full power. As the current hit the console, it was like it hit Adri as well. He fell to the ground, clutching his head in agony.

With a creak, the lab began to drop out of sky. As we fell, the walls and floor lost their transparency. Soon they were white and opaque again. I could no longer see through them, but I knew what was coming. My stomach dropped. Yara slept. Adri writhed in pain.

We were about to crash down into the Zoo.

Chapter Twenty-Two

GOODBYE

I held on tight to Adri with one hand and gripped the console with the other. I closed my eyes, felt the impact, and heard crashing and breaking all around me.

I opened my eyes slowly. Miraculously, Adri and I were still alive. The lab's walls and floor had long cracks and gashes, but it was still in one piece and relatively upright.

The memory-stick still buzzed and sparked in the console, sending the lab's systems haywire. Yara's cylinder slid open, sloshing her into the room with a wave of the green liquid and disconnected lines from her cryotube. She groaned and struggled to her feet in the mess. Then she scanned the room, taking in my terrified face and Adri's seizure, with one look.

"Five minutes to self-destruct," the Centre announced.

Great. Of all things, that was still working.

"Run," Yara commanded, leaping over the console. She yanked the glitching memory-stick out and jabbed it like a spear into one side of the lab, trying to make a burning, jagged hole wide enough to get through.

Apparently, when it was turned up all the way, whatever energy the memory-stick used was like electricity gone mad. Small bolts of lightning flew from it everywhere. I curled up next to Adri, trying not to get hit.

The damaged console rumbled. It flashed, screeched, then exploded, slamming Adri and I to opposite ends of the lab. I moaned and got up slowly, dragging myself back over to Adri, as Yara continued to wreak havoc on the lab wall.

Adri was dazed, with a bump the size of an egg growing on his head, but his eyes were his. He stared up at me and tried to speak, but nothing came out.

"It's okay. We'll be okay," I whispered to him, trying to believe it myself.

I heard metallic shrieks outside, drawing closer

to the ship, a sound I'd never forget.

"X!" Yara hissed.

"Four minutes to self-destruct."

We didn't have much time to get out of here. Yara picked up the pace, focusing on carving her way through a crack in one of the ship's walls. I could hear the skittering clash and screams of enraged X outside. How were we going to escape that way?

Just before she squeezed through the opening into the rising shrieks of the X, Yara turned back to look at me. Her braids swirled around her like flying shadows, her eyes fierce like a hawk's.

"Go," she warned me sharply, "and don't ever come back."

Then she stepped outside.

"Three minutes to self-destruct."

Hopefully, we could slip through while Yara distracted the X. I knew she could take care of herself and get to safety. It was my job to get Adri out. I reached under his arms and tried to drag him toward the opening. He was heavy for such a tall, skinny kid. He was losing consciousness, but still trying to speak. Without his legs, we wouldn't get far, but I had to try.

"Samaan Bay," he whispered, "now."

Didn't I wish.

"Two minutes to self-destruct," the Centre blared.

Fires were spreading all over the lab, where Yara had gone to town with the memory-stick. The exploding console had blown more holes in the walls. This place was falling apart around us. I could hear more explosions in the compound outside and the clash, shrieks, and clatter of Yara fighting the X just beyond the walls of the lab.

How were we going to get through all of that, over the Zoo's giant wall and out into the forest?

Maybe I should call for Yara to come back, but that would attract the X too. She was the only thing keeping them at bay.

Adri passed out. Smashing the console and knocking his head in the crash had seemed to break his tie to the SYM. I didn't know if it would last, but we couldn't stick around to find out. I tried again to pull him across the floor toward another one of the narrow openings. We made it a few more feet before I had to stop. I was exhausted, but I couldn't give up. We'd come this far. I couldn't give up now, but I didn't have the strength to keep fighting.

"One minute... to self-destruct." The Centre's warning stuttered through the noise.

I sank to the ground next to Adri with my head bowed, trying to take one more deep breath.

There was a loud beeping noise that grew faster and more threatening. This was it. The Zoo was about to blow. I braced myself and held Adri close.

Then I heard it – something like drums. Next to me, a large web began to form in the air.

Different voices – squeaky, gravelly, loud, low, high, hoarse and hairy - leaked through the web.

"You hear that beeping Neesha? Move faster nah!"

"Kemi, we doh have all day!"

"Watch your angles ladies, keep the corners tight..."

"Faheema, is more webbing we need, not a geometry lesson."

"Rosa Maria, ent I tell you that common-sense make before book?"

"And it not all that common."

"Well, Satine, finally you get something right. Now move your legs before this whole place explode!"

"Kya-ha-ha! Allyuh fraid to dead or what? When I dead bury mih clothes!" A deep voice burst out singing.

"Doh want nobody to cry for me," the other voices chimed in.

"When I dead bury mih clothes!"

"Put everything in the cemetery!" It was a call and response.

The drums beat faster.

"Sing and work allyuh, sing and work."

It was a cackling, complaining chorus of spiders. I was never happier to hear their crazy voices.

They sprang through the now translucent portal with Cap'n Peg at the head, her mechanical arm whining in my ears: "Girlie, is time to clear out, unless you want to be cinders and smoke!"

Through the portal, I could see a leaf-strewn path and smell the clean scent of leaves mixed with cool earth. In seconds, the spiders grabbed Adri and I by our arms, legs and hair, and began dragging us through the web.

Wait. What about...

"Yara!" I screamed.

We couldn't leave her. I could hear her cries over the screech of the X outside the lab.

"Yara!"

She'd saved our lives. If I could just buy her a little more time, she could escape through the portal with us.

"Crazy Two-Legs," the spiders shouted.

"Leave she, yes," one advised.

I fought against the spiders' hairy legs, but Cap'n Peg grabbed me with her mechanical limb and yanked me through the portal, just as I heard and saw a bright boom.

Immediately, it was quiet, as if someone had suddenly switched off the TV.

Adri and I were lying down on a small, paved trail that went through the bamboo cathedral. I knew this spot. It was close to the house Jake had found for me, Mum and Baby T, in Samaan Bay.

Here in the 'cathedral', the rods of bamboo had grown so tall that they curved over the path in an arched ceiling, accented by patches of light and sky. They creaked and swayed above me. The towering stalks bent their heads together like old friends whispering secrets. Green and yellow leaves, like long thin tongues, muttered and fluttered in the breeze. Out of sight, in the bushes, small creatures rustled by, as if late for a secret rendezvous.

Once the spiders pulled us away from the fading web, they swung away from Adri and I, up into the trees. But they didn't go far. They seemed to be hanging around, waiting for something. Even more strange, they were quiet, looking at each other expectantly.

"How long this going to take?" one of them muttered, but the others shushed her.

Cap'n Peg shut them all up by closing the claws of her mechanical arm together with a loud snap.

Tears burned my cheeks. They dripped down onto Adri's still face. We were back in Samaan Bay, but we'd left Yara behind.

"Just go! Leave us alone!" I yelled.

I should be thanking the spiders for saving me and Adri, but I was shaking. I couldn't stand any of this anymore.

"Not our call girlie," Cap'n Peg avoided my eyes, "and too besides, this ain't about Yara, or you."

Then I realized that the spiders weren't even looking at me. All their round black eyes were trained on Adri. He was moving.

Adri mumbled and sat up slowly. He stared at me with a haunted expression, as if I were just coming into focus. To my relief, the red eyes of the SYM were gone.

I scanned his face. "Adri?"

Was it really him?

"Zo, I'm so sorry," he stammered, "...my parents!"

299

"Adri, your parents are..." I tried reminding him of what I'd seen in his memory – how they'd fought for him to the end.

"No!" he shook his head. "One of the Council's machines... it took me and my parents. Came up from underwater and yanked us out of the sea. Brought us all to the Zoo!"

I froze. His parents really were still alive.

Adri trembled as if he were cold. "The Council has Ma and Dad. They said if I didn't let them put the chip in my head, I'd never see them again."

"They'd have left the Zoo by now," Cap'n Peg cut in, gently shaking her head.

Adri scrambled to his feet. "Wherever they are, I have to get back to the Council, or they'll make my parents pay."

"What?" I shouted. "Are you crazy? You can't go back! They'll turn you into the SYM again. Make you do whatever they want! You can't..."

Adri looked at me in silence and I knew.

"I have to go back," he answered, "I can't leave them."

I thought of his parents' faces on the boat that day – the light in their eyes whenever they'd looked at him.

300

Of course he was going back for them.

I could see on his face how scared he was, and how sure.

After everything we'd been through, I knew what courage looked like.

"Good," Cap'n Peg interrupted, "because our Boss don't want to have to explain to the Council how we lost one of their top assets."

The other spiders erupted in agreement; "You got that right! This eh Peter pay for Paul and Paul pay for all! We not about to be blamed for you, sir. No way!"

I bit back tears. This was hard enough for Adri. He shouldn't have to see me cry.

"What about Zo?" Adri asked the spiders suddenly, suspiciously. "What happens to her?"

Cap'n Peg looked at me with something close to sympathy. "Don't worry. She gets to go home... for now."

I couldn't even feel relieved.

Cap'n Peg said softly to Adri, "Time to go."

She pointed between two nearby trees. When had the spiders made that new web? It was already translucent inside. This time, I couldn't see where it led to. It didn't sound like the war zone of the Zoo. I could hear car horns blaring, engines growling, music blasting and the street noise of a city, but everything inside the web was hidden by a thick fog.

That didn't stop the spiders. They jumped right in, shouting; "Later 'gators! Hasta never! Sayonara! Ciao! We gone!"

Cap'n Peg shook my weak hand with her mechanical claw. "You're a good one girlie. See you soon." She grinned wisely and disappeared into the web. What were the odds that I'd ever see them again?

Adri looked at me, but I couldn't meet his eyes. I tried to find the right thing to say.

I felt his warm dry hand press into mine.

"Bye Zo," I heard him whisper, then he was gone.

Chapter Twenty-Three

START

I sank down where the web and my friend had been, fists clenched in the dirt, tears scorching my face.

Suddenly, I was aware of something behind me.

I swung around and there was Ms. Kofi, standing with both hands on the hips of her green and gold ankara dress.

The 'I told you so' look on her face made my blood boil.

"Well look at that. You made it," she pointed out drily.

"No thanks to you!" I screamed.

"Watch it child," Ms. K raised her eyebrows, taking a step towards me.

I remembered that she didn't take rudeness lightly. It was true that she'd sent me that mind-mail back on the hill. Her spider-crew had jumped in to save us more than once, even pulling us out of the Zoo in the nick of time. Most of all, she was a giant spider posing as a woman, so maybe I should watch my mouth – but I was done being yanked around like a yo-yo on a string.

"Ms. Kofi," I said stiffly, pointing at the path through the bamboo cathedral, "I'm going home."

"Listen, child," she leaned forward urgently, "we don't have much time. The Council will say that a fire caused old gas tanks at the 'abandoned research labs' to explode." She smiled grimly. "You and I both know the truth."

I felt like throwing up. "What about Adri, his parents, Yara? Can you help them?"

"That is no longer your problem," Ms. K shook her head, her elaborate headtie staying firmly in place.

Her eyes were dark, wrinkled, and impossible to read.

"Your problem is that I have to wipe your memory. Now."

"No..." I inched away.

"Council's orders. I've got to wipe everything back to when you first ran away. You and everyone else will think you were just lost in the forest and hit your head. You won't remember the rest of what happened over the last few days."

Ms. K slid a memory-stick smoothly from her dress. It jolted to life with blue and silver light.

I backed away from her, spinning from side to side. If I ran, I wouldn't get very far.

"Do it then!" I shouted defiantly. "You're all spies and pawns for the Council anyway! The spiders, Kala, you... Adri." I choked on his name, tears blinding my eyes. "I don't want to remember any of it!"

Ms. K moved in, the light from the memory-stick flashing in her eyes. "Child, what you know?"

She seemed to grow to three or four times her height. "The Council is not done with you... with any of us. Them so, is never done."

The sun shone down through the ceiling of bamboo, covering Ms. K with black and

gold stripes. "When they're ready for you, they will come to take you away for training. Months from now, a year, who knows?"

The shadows around Ms. K looked like arms unfolding. Her voice dropped to a deep rumble – the sound of ancient grinding stone. "And when that time comes child, there'll be no turning back."

My mind and body froze. There was no way out.

Ms. K grabbed me by the arm and yanked me toward her, muttering in my ear, "So watch this."

****

I opened my eyes in a dark place. It smelled like wood and gobar smoke. My body felt strange. It wasn't my own. My back was bent. I couldn't straighten up all the way. I looked at my gnarled, lined hands. They belonged to an old woman, not to me. They held a small flambeau lamp, made of a green glass bottle wrapped in cloth and filled with what smelt like coconut oil, with a cloth wick floating inside. It burned with a low, flickering light. I was in a small space, between earth walls held together by a thick web of rambling roots.

Somehow, in a second, I had ended up underground, surrounded by the roots of great trees.

"Yancy, we don't have much time," my lips said in a voice that wasn't my own.

It was Ms. K's voice. This was her body. I was inside one of Ms. Kofi's memories. And I wasn't alone.

Out of the darkness, a raffia hat emerged, then a sharp face and neat body dressed in colours so bright that they stood out, even in this dark hole.

It was Mr. Yancy, the old man from the market, wearing his magical coat. He grinned at Ms. Kofi; a mischievous, daring smile. "I know sis, but this is the one."

His multicoloured, mismatched coat fluttered into the shape of a baby elephant's head and nodded wisely in agreement.

"See, even Sesa thinks so!" Mr. Yancy pointed out triumphantly.

So, the coat's name was Sesa. My heart sank as I pictured the last time I'd seen it, being dragged to the Zoo by a swarm of spiders.

I tried to focus on what was happening. Wait. Mr. Yancy had called Ms. Kofi 'sis'! Were they really brother and sister? Then why had he warned me against her?

I felt a mix of affection and irritation flood Ms. K's body as she looked at her brother. Just like the times I'd fallen into other people's memories, she seemed unaware of my presence, far less my confusion. All her focus was on Mr. Yancy and what he was about to tell her.

"What is it now brother? What magic weapon to bring down the Council? This better not be another one of your wild deer chases!" She schooled him like only a big sister could. "We don't have any more time for dead ends."

"No sis, hear me out," Mr. Yancy begged, "this is it. This is what we've been looking for. The weapon that can finally help get the Council off our backs."

What was it – his coat, Sesa? It had taken the shape of a monkey and was making faces at Ms. K from behind Old Yancy's back. She ignored it studiously. I pictured the magical coat getting dragged away by the spiders in front of Adri's and my eyes. This plan of theirs clearly hadn't worked.

Ms. K hesitated. I felt doubt and hope fight for space inside her body.

I struggled with my own thoughts. Something powerful enough to bring down the Council. What could it be? My head spun trying to figure it out. I was tired of being trapped in another memory, tossed around by other people's plans.

Ms. K was on edge and so was I.

"Whatever it is," she argued, "we might have to give it up to the Council first – make sure they don't suspect me. Then we can use it to bring them down when the time is right."

"No!" Old Yancy shook his head violently. "I am sick of running. We should use it right away. No more hiding and skulking around in the dark!"

"But brother, we must be careful, learn more about this weapon. Take our time. The Council has to keep thinking we hate each other. If they find out we're working together, you know what they'll do! And if this weapon doesn't save us, then what?" Ms. K hissed. "All these years of searching for a way to get out from under the Council's thumb, gone to waste."

"I hear you Sister," Yancy pleaded, "but this is it... You know I have the nose for sensing power."

Finally, Ms. K sighed. "Okay then, what is it? What is this weapon that's going to end our secret war?"

Mr. Yancy grinned proudly. His teeth flashed in the dimness. His golden eyes glowed brighter than the light of the flambeau held high in Ms. K's hands.

"Not what..." he said quietly, "whom."

I could feel the shock course through Ms. K's body.

"Her name," Mr. Yancy murmured, "is Zo."

****

Wait. What? That couldn't be right.

I blinked and was back in the bamboo cathedral – dappled sunlight falling on my face. Ms. K had let go of my arm, but she was still right up in my face. She smelled of bay leaves, cut grass, fresh mud, and something else feral and strange. She was snarling and I was shaking, stuck in place, shocked by everything I'd just seen and heard.

Then with the tiniest of breaths, barely moving her lips, Ms. K whispered to me, "Play along."

That's when I realised that she had the memory-stick, crackling and buzzing, against my left temple.

"Ahhhh!" I screamed and tried to run away, but she pressed one of her feet down hard on mine and held the memory-stick firmly to my head.

There was a blinding flash.

All my memories of Adri, his treachery and bravery, were going to be sucked out of me; erased in a moment. Everything we'd been through together would be lost. Those memories dashed across my mind like scenes from a movie. I tried to hold on to each and every one.

"It's more painful if you fight it," Ms. K warned me loudly.

I whimpered. Then I realised that I didn't feel any electric shock, any pain.

In fact, despite all the memory-stick's bright lights and noise, there was nothing but a tickling sensation on the side of my face. My eyes widened and my mouth dropped open. Was this some kind of game - another test from the Council?

Then it hit me that I could remember the Council and Adri. I could remember everything. I trembled and cried out, but this time, not in pain.

Tears ran down my face. I shook like a leaf in a storm. To anyone watching, it would look like I was in shock and pain. I realized now that that was a good thing.

Ms. K wasn't erasing my memories. She was only pretending to erase them, to fool the Council.

This must mean that she believed what her brother Yancy had said: that I was the one to help them take the Council down. Now, it was my turn to play along.

Ms. K turned the memory-stick off and slipped it back into the folds of her wrapper.

"Zo?" she said carefully.

I kept my face blank for a moment, then shook myself slowly, as if coming back to life.

"M-Ms. K?" I stuttered. "Is that you?"

"Zo!" She raised her hands to the sky. "You're alive!"

I looked down. Somehow, I was back in my old shoes and clothes. They were torn and filthy, as if they'd never been washed at Yara's home.

"I ran away... Got lost in the forest," I stammered, "followed the river to find my way out. I-I think I hit my head somewhere... I can't remember..."

If I wanted to get out of here, I'd better keep going along with her plan to make it seem like I'd lost all my memories of the robotic gnats, Cap'n Peg and the spiders, the X, Yara, Kala, Adri, and most of all, the Council.

"You poor child!" Ms. K cried, propping me up by my shoulders, careful not to touch my bare skin and trigger another fall into her memory.

"What were you thinking?" She scolded me gently. "Your mother is a wreck. She can't sleep, she barely eats. Your father and Jake go out every day to look for you. In fact, they're searching for you right now."

Da... I knew he'd come find me. Hot tears burned my eyes. I'd almost forgotten why I'd done this in

312

the first place. It all seemed so silly now. Mum and Da, Jake and Tayo – my family, old and new: all I wanted was to give them a huge hug. I pictured Da and Jake out searching for me day after day, never giving up hope.

With Ms. Kofi and Old Yancy's help, I'd keep searching too; until I found Adri and his parents.

Ms. K was fussing over me while throwing veiled warnings my way, like, "I shouldn't have taken my eyes off you for a second on that road by the smelter. I'll be watching you like a hawk from now on."

I needed to be careful with her. Was she on my side, or was I just a tool for her to use against the Council?

Either way, two could play that game. I was scared, but I had something stronger than fear now, and I didn't just mean my gift.

I needed to find Adri again.

I caught the sharp smell of smoke from somewhere in the mountains behind us. Black wisps of ash came dancing on the wind.

"Forest fire," Ms. K said, her eyes filled with something like pain.

So, the Council had done it. They had destroyed the Research Centre and set part of the forest and swamp on fire – covering their tracks.

We had to hurry to warn the village, in case the fire came close. They would collect buckets and truckloads of water, send for the fire brigade in the nearest town; doing everything in their power to keep the flames from spreading and destroying everything in their path.

A soft breeze swirled around me, salty from the sea, pushing back the bitter scent of smoke. It set the rows of bamboo, in all their shapes and shades, talking and moving as one.

"Who are you?" Adri had asked me when we first met, after we'd made it out of the river.

Whatever happened next, I was going to find out.

ZO AND ADRI WILL BE BACK IN 2023...

BOOK TWO IS COMING

ACKNOWLEDGMENTS

This book only exists because of so many people. It's impossible to thank you all by name here, but you know who you are and the space you hold in my heart. Thank you Jesus, for making all things new. A special thank-you to my parents and siblings, who continue to support the dream in every way. Thanks to my grandparents, especially my grandmothers, for their faith, love, and courage. My sister-friends, prayer-warrior aunties, uncles, cousins, and extended family on all sides. There is no book, or me, without you.

My not-so-little one: thank you for all your gifts. To the doctors and nurses who were involved in your care, and the family, friends, faculty and students who were so supportive during your illness, words will never be enough.

To the teachers and fellow-students at every place that I've studied – NYU, LSU, UEA, and the precious people at Bates College – thank you for the lessons you taught me. Thank you to the Booker Prize Foundation for making the MA in Creative Writing at the University of East Anglia possible. It was a magical time. To the writing mentors and organisers of the Cropper Foundation Writers' Workshop, the Bocas Lit

Fest, the St. James Writing Room, the West Indian Literature Conference, the Callaloo Journal Creative Writing Workshop in Barbados, and the always welcoming Community of Writers: thank you for the space to create and connect.

To my fellow and sister-writers around the world, especially those working in Trinidad & Tobago and the wider Caribbean, keep the faith on this often circuitous journey of writing. Thank you to every editor and journal that has ever published or awarded a prize to my work, including the Small Axe Journal, Moko Magazine, the Center for Fiction, The Haunted Tropics, the &NOW Awards, the Commonwealth Short Story Prize, and the inspiring anthology New Daughters of Africa. You renewed my hope at key moments.

Heartfelt thanks to my groundbreaking publisher, Knights Of, including managing director Aimée, my brilliant editor Eishar, creative director Marssaié and everyone who makes up their team of superheroes. You make room for books and authors that are rarely seen and are true champions of children's literature.

Thank you Isobel, my children's book agent at Curtis Brown. I look forward to a bright future together. Thanks to the talented Tasia, who made beautiful cover art. And the teams at ed.pr, Bounce Sales & Marketing, New Leaf Literary, and the ILA agency, for continuing to share ZO with the world and wonderful readers like you!

Alake Pilgrim

AUTHOR

Alake Pilgrim writes from the uncanny islands of the Caribbean, where people are connected to Africa, India, China, the Americas, Europe, and the Middle East. She has an MA in Creative Writing from the University of East Anglia, thanks to the Booker Prize Foundation Scholarship, an MA in Latin American & Caribbean Studies from New York University, and a BA in Politics from Bates College.

Her stories have twice won the regional prize for the Americas in the Commonwealth Short Story Competition. They have been published by The Center for Fiction in New York, the Small Axe Journal, *The Haunted Tropics* edited by Martin Munro (UWI Press), and in the groundbreaking international anthology *New Daughters of Africa*, edited by Margaret Busby (Myriad Editions and Amistad/HarperCollins). *Zo and the Forest of Secrets* is Alake's first book and the start of her middle-grade fantasy series.

Tasia Graham

ILLUSTRATOR

Tasia Graham explores bold, atmospheric, narrative illustration, using her colourful pallet and fluid, stylized drawing techniques. Working in both digital format and traditional painting, Tasia explores womanhood, culture, and identity, depicting moods and scenes formed into illustrative storytelling.

Tasia's work has been shortlisted for the Penguin Design Awards, and has worked with Moonpig, The University of Arts London and many others.

KO

KNIGHTS OF

KNIGHTS OF is a multi award-winning inclusive publisher focused on bringing underrepresented voices to the forefront of commercial children's publishing. With a team led by women of colour, and an unwavering focus on their intended readership for each book, Knights Of works to engage with gatekeepers across the industry, including booksellers, teachers and librarians, and supports non-traditional community spaces with events, outreach, marketing and partnerships.